Hannah

The Brides of Pine Creek

By

Georgina Sellwood

Chapter One

What will my life be like in Pine Creek, Lord?

Raw, icy fear gripped Hannah as she waited at the railcar door.

Steeling herself for what lay ahead, she nodded to the conductor to open the exit. She stepped onto the metal deck at the end of the car. He placed a stool at the foot of the stairs for her to descend from the train.

The town folk let out a raucous cheer for Hannah and the seven other mail-order-brides.

Tendrils of hair whipped across her vision, and her skirt billowed in the fierce prairie wind. The land lay flat for miles in all directions, a wasteland of brown waiting for spring to bring it back to life.

Could Harland already be here, in Pine Creek, waiting to silence her?

Fear tightened bands around her chest, and she held her breath as she scanned the assembled crowd for familiar features. One by one, she checked each man's countenance.

She breathed a sigh of relief. There were no recognizable faces watching, waiting. She was safe, for now.

She straightened her hair and brushed at her blue wool skirt, plastered on a smile she didn't feel, and descended to the scarred, wooden platform of the rail station.

The crowd cheered and clapped another welcome.

The escorts for the trip, Mr. and Mrs. Frank Clarke, stood waiting to make introductions.

Before they could do so, a man with a large round stomach stepped forward. As he shook Hannah's hand, it disappeared in the man's meaty grip.

"Hello, and welcome to our town. I'm Jim Davis, the mayor of Pine Creek."

The Clarkes stood back, openmouthed. Hannah understood their apparent horror at this man's lack of manners.

"Nice to meet you, sir. I'm Hannah Waaaalt . . . uh, Hannah Wall."

She gave her brightest smile, hoping he would ignore her hesitation. He turned to the younger man beside him with neatly cropped brown hair. "This is our pastor, Marcus Attwood."

"Hello, Miss Wall. We're so glad you've come to find a husband and make your home here." He shook her hand in a friendly greeting.

The crowd around them cheered again as the next bride appeared. Hannah moved down the line and met more of the town dignitaries. The last one was a broad-shouldered man wearing a worn white Stetson.

"Welcome, miss, I'm Sheriff Mitch Campbell." He shone a warm smile down on her from his handsome face. "We've arranged to take you by buggy to the hotel. Step this way, and this young man'll help you."

Hannah lingered a little too long on Mitch Campbell's face, drawn by the magnetism in his dark eyes.

Could he be one of the grooms?

A lad with curly red hair in his late teens helped her into a fancy black carriage. "I'm Scott, Miss. If there's anything you need while you're here in town, please let me know." Hannah smiled and thanked him.

She twisted her mother's linen gloves in her lap and took furtive glances around for recognizable faces. A quick flash came to mind, of Harland standing over his poor dead mother, the pillow from the dead woman's bed held firmly over her frail face. She shuddered remembering her shock and horror. She knew now what he was capable of. What her fate would be if he found her.

When all eight of the brides had come through the gauntlet, they rode by buggy to the hotel. Her companions on the short ride feasted their eyes on the dressmaker's window as they rumbled passed.

"Look at the pretty calico and muslin in all different colors," exclaimed Melanie.

"Oh, hats and dresses too," Victoria chimed in.

Next, the mercantile caught their interest with windows lined with various items--serving bowls, china, and glassware.

"Ladies, see that exquisite serving bowl. I hope I find a husband rich enough to buy me that," Victoria gasped in delight.

Hannah fought to rid herself of the trauma and fear the memory of Harland inflicted.

Then a pungent odor assailed her, and she covered her nose with her hand. She glanced to the right. They passed the blacksmith shop and livery stable. Her nose wrinkled in revulsion. She held her breath and hoped her breakfast would stay down.

"What is that smell?" Victoria's nose wrinkled in disgust.

"It's horse dung, city girl." Melanie grinned.

"I'll avoid that side of the street." Hannah turned away.

They pulled up to the hotel, a two-story wooden building with a balcony stretched across the front. Hannah followed the others onto the porch and listened to the mayor give his speech from the doorway.

"Ladies, we'll be putting you up here until you come to decide which of our fine men you'd like to marry." He coughed into a handkerchief. "Tomorrow night, we'll have a reception at the town hall. There, you can meet the potential grooms and our town folk."

As the brides entered the hotel, Hannah heard one of the men say, "That little one will never last out here. Look how pale she is."

"I'm stronger than I look, mister," Hannah mumbled under her breath and strode a little taller.

Hannah followed a boyish-looking bride, Bernice, into the hotel, where a friendly woman with graying hair and a wide smile met them in the foyer.

"Hello, I'm Nellie. I hope you enjoy your stay here."

"Thank you for having us." Melanie ran a pudgy hand through her blond hair.

Nellie ushered the brides into the dining room and offered them refreshments while the men took their bags upstairs. As Hannah sat at a table sipping tea from a china cup, she watched the other women. Most were of average height; the boyish-looking one, who wore trousers and boots, was tallest. The most beautiful was the one called Lily with the strawberry blonde hair. A couple of cascading curls had escaped from under her hat and framed Lily's pretty oval face.

The mayor chose that moment to enter the room and make an announcement. "Ladies, we have your rooms ready. Please partner up, and head upstairs when you're finished here."

Hannah went to pair up with Lily, but she was at another table. "Sorry, I've agreed to room with Mary."

Undaunted, she tried Melanie next. "Sorry, my partner just went up to pick out our room."

Looking around for another choice her eyes fell on Bernice. In the mad scramble, she was the only bride left and stood forlornly with her arms crossed wiping at her hook-nose. She reminded Hannah of a solitary bandy rooster with her frizzy red hair. They looked at one another knowing they would be roommates.

"Come on Bernice, let's finish our tea and then get settled." Hannah smiled and picked up her cup.

Later, as she climbed the old, worn staircase, Hannah rolled her eyes as Bernice's nasal voice droned. This was the bride who had been loud and obnoxious on the train chattering up a storm while others tried to sleep.

Nellie led them to a cozy corner room facing the street. A bed covered by a green and white Irish Chain quilt sat in the center of an oriental rug. A double mahogany dresser rested against one wall.

Once in their room, Bernice chatted incessantly as she unpacked her belongings.

"Oh, Hannah, isn't this just the most exciting day of your entire life?" Hannah stood at the window and surveyed the street below.

"Yes, this is exciting, all right," she muttered under her breath.

"I can't wait to meet the grooms. I hope one that has lots of animals will marry me." Bernice chattered on and on until Hannah had to get away. Her babble gave Hannah a headache.

"I need to ask the hotel owner about ah--towels." She exited quickly before Bernice could decide to come with her.

Her shoes clicked a swift rhythm across the foyer and out the front door. Worried Bernice would follow, she rushed down the wooden boardwalk. As she bolted across the first side street, the sound of fast-approaching horses reached her too late.

A man's voice yelled, "Look out!"

She whirled to get out of the way as a large buckboard came straight at her.

The driver yelled, "Whoa!"

In her haste, her feet tangled in her long skirt, and she toppled face first into the street onto the hard-packed ground. When she landed, the air in her lungs hissed out in one long whoosh.

Hannah struggled for breath, and spit out foul-tasting dirt. Her chest, arms and face throbbed from the impact. Familiar-looking boots came into her limited view and panic gripped her. The tooled-in curly cues on the boots looked like Harland's.

He's found me.

She rolled into a ball, covered her head with both arms and waited for those boots to begin their assault.

Then an unknown baritone voice said, "Lady, you're lucky to be alive."

An unforgiving hand clamped onto her upper arm and roughly hauled Hannah to her feet. As she came up, she realized the person who wore the boots was not Harland, but a very annoyed stranger. Windblown black hair hung over one eye. A day's worth of black stubble covered his chin. His expression was one of irritation and perhaps anger at how close she had come to causing him to run her down.

"You about scared me to death, lady. You wanna die?" He peered down his eyes shaded under the brim of his hat.

Still in the grip of her original fear, Hannah trembled uncontrollably.

She crossed her arms over her chest in a protective stance and stared into the man's frightening black eyes.

"Miss, you best sit down. You're as white as a sheet on my Mama's clothesline."

"I'm all right," she said just above a whisper, and tried to shake the man off. It was like having Harland right there. He was the last person she wanted help from right now. Everything about this stranger reminded her of Harland, his flashing black eyes and unruly black hair. His towering height and whip-thin frame.

All the fear she had carried on the trip across country lingered right at the surface, and all she wanted was to let the tears go. Her eyes stung and her throat hurt with the effort to hold them back. Her chin quivered. She hoped he wouldn't notice.

He stood much too close, making her feel insignificant and small. The smell of animal dung wafted off his clothes. Maybe this mail-order-bride idea was foolish. The last thing she wanted was to marry someone who smelled like him.

Forced by the man's strong, sun-browned, work-roughened hands, she was made to sit on the edge of the wooden boardwalk. Still feeling the near-death fright, Hannah huddled, suddenly cold and trembling, relieved to get off her shaky legs. A lone tear escaped despite her best effort to hold it back. It made a trail down her dirty cheek.

When she looked up, the stranger had left and a crowd of men with concerned faces stood around her.

"I'm fine now. Thank you, everyone." She touched her mouth and discovered dirt from the street still stuck to her face.

In Boston, I would never let my hands get this dirty.

Her cheeks heated as she realized the entire time the stranger harangued her, she'd had half the street plastered to her skin. As she allowed one of the men to help her up, she angrily swiped at the grime.

Oh please Lord, just let me find a man who can make me feel safe.

Chapter Two

Hannah allowed the kind-hearted Pastor Attwood to walk her to the hotel. He was the one person she recognized as a town dignitary who offered to help her back to the hotel.

"Who was that wild driver who almost ran me over?" She shivered remembering the earlier trauma.

Pastor Attwood looked down at her and smiled. "That would be Cage McCormack."

Never having heard the name Cage in Boston, she asked, "Cage. What kind of a name is that?"

"Micajah, is his proper name. It's Scottish."

"His parents were from Scotland, then?" she asked, her interest peaked.

"Yes, both of them, I believe. He lives with his mother on a cattle farm about ten miles outside of town." He took her arm as they crossed a side street.

"Has his father passed on?"

"No, Miss, but that isn't something for idle discussion." He directed her around some pot-holes.

"Hmm." Her brows drew together. She fiddled with her gloves, but didn't press him. She filed the information away to perhaps ask Nellie or someone else later.

After she cleaned her face at the pump, Hannah rested in a white wicker rocker on the hotel's porch while Pastor Attwood went to get her a cup of hot tea. She bit her nails and rocked while she waited, ever-watchful for a familiar face passing by.

Several men looked in to catch a glance of a bride or two. Their searching gazes unnerved her.

Hannah didn't feel out of harm's way here. She needed to find a safer place to hide. Putting distance between her and Harland helped, but she still thought there was a chance he could trace her here.

The young pastor came back with a tray of tea and dainties. She took the tray from him and placed it on the white wicker table between them.

The familiar aroma of Darjeeling tea from India wafted as she poured. "Thank you."

After Hannah poured his tea, she hesitated briefly and then picked up the small silver spoon and stirred spoonfuls of sugar into the hot black drink. Then she tipped the rich cream into her cup until the liquid turned a caramel color.

Sitting back with a satisfied smile she sipped her tea. No one would ever tell her how she should take her tea again.

A dark-haired man with a star pinned to his chest sauntered onto the porch.

"Sheriff Mitch Campbell, you've met Hannah Wall." He gestured from one to the other.

A solid hand gripped Hannah's. "Pleased to see you again. I hear you had a close call earlier."

"I'm fine now, thank you."

She liked the sheriff's size. He was a big, solid man with a friendly smile. His dark eyes held warmth as he took her hand.

"Please be assured that we all want you to be safe here, Miss Wall."

You have no idea how much I want that, too.

Hannah gave him a grateful smile. "Thank you, Sheriff. It was my fault, really. I should have watched where I was going. It was clumsy of me."

The sheriff leaned against the porch rail. "Everyone will soon be asking you. So I might as well beat them to it. What are you looking for in a husband?"

Heat warmed her face. She hated to lie. But knew lying would be the only thing that kept her safe. If any of these men found out, she was in truth hiding from Harland. They could turn her over immediately. What would she do then? No, lying was essential.

She did not come here to marry. This trip was paid for by the grooms and a cheap way to get a lot of distance between herself and Harland. "I'm not fond of cattle, so a wheat farmer, I suppose," she responded, suppressing a grin.

Mitch frowned. "Life on a farm can be very remote and lonely."

The further from town the better.

A plan began to form in the back of her mind. Yes, out of town would be safer.

"I'm a good cook and can keep house, so I think I would find plenty to occupy my time."

An uncomfortable silence ensued. The sound of bees buzzing in the shrubs beside the porch drew her attention and made Hannah squirm.

The flowering bushes shielded the shaded porch from the street beyond, and the scent of lilacs was a welcome reminder of Boston.

As she gazed out over the street, several men peered at her through the branches of the nearby shrubbery. Any one of them could have been sent here by Harland. She took one last sip of her now tepid tea.

"Excuse me, gentlemen. I think I'll go freshen up. Thank you for making me feel sa--welcome." She extended her hand. "It was nice to see you again, Sheriff." Their eyes met and she gave him a genuine smile.

"I'll see you tomorrow at the reception." He doffed his hat and his dark eyes followed her.

The men still hovered on the street and an uncomfortable feeling chased her inside. She kept to the shadows with her face averted as she hurried to the safety of her room.

***

Hannah looked into a propped-up hand mirror in the hotel kitchen, pinning her auburn hair on top of her head. Her heart beat a happy rhythm in anticipation of the coming reception. Bernice stood behind her, with a curling iron warmed on the stove. They planned to make ringlets cascade from Hannah's top knot.

"You're gonna be the best lookin' bride-to-be there," Bernice said in her nasal voice.

"We'll spruce you up too," Hannah reassured her. "I have cream that will help to hide your freckles. And we'll style your hair as well."

She did her best to braid Bernice's wiry red locks and coil it at the crown of her head. She finger curled her bangs along the brow.

They finished with their hair and with a flat iron began pressing their dresses.

Bernice tested the bottom of the iron to see if it was ready. "Ouch."

"Careful it's not too hot. That filmy brown material won't need too much heat." She thought the brown would look nice with Bernice's eyes. "Don't scorch it. The other dress you brought won't look as nice with your hair."

Next, Hannah ironed the dress she had chosen, an empire-waist in pink with long belled sleeves. She had two others but she favored this one.

"Those sleeves are wonderful, they look positively Victorian," Bernice gushed.

When other girls started crowding into the kitchen, they finished and left to dress in their room.

They laughed and joked as the excitement of the coming evening mounted. After a touch of rose water behind each ear, she followed Bernice downstairs to wait for their carriage ride to the town hall.

The other brides joined them a few minutes later. The buggies arrived and drove them the short distance to the reception, which was at the far end of the street near the railroad station. The town hall looked typical, but Hannah could see that the citizens took a lot of pride in its appearance.

Miniature gardens grew along the front on either side of the door. The baby plants looked freshly watered and weeded.

Scott, the redheaded lad, stepped up. "Hello, may I walk you in?"

The mayor stood nearby, nodding his approval.

As Scott escorted her out of the buggy and up the front steps, she noticed a freshly painted sign beside the door: Pine Creek, Town Hall. This homey setting moved her.

Help me make this pleasant, quiet town my home, Lord.

As Scott led her to the far end of the room where eight chairs sat in a row, her fingernails dug into his arm as she scanned the assembled faces. As she took her seat and thanked him, she tried to relax. No reason to worry, she told herself. Would she ever be able to relax completely?

One of the grooms caught the attention of a bride by taking her a glass of punch. Hannah watched as this spurred the other men to do the same thing, and before she could catch a breath, men made a mad dash to the punch bowl, sloshing the juice all over the floor in their urgency.

One poor man slipped in the sticky, sweet concoction and went down on his backside. Several men suddenly stood in front of her offering her glasses of the pink punch. One had an old,

grizzled face with a gray beard.
Another had a sweet innocent smile, but
bad breath she could smell from a
distance. She took the glass from a
young man about her age.

With so many single men vying for
the attention of the eight women,
pushing and shoving had ensued. Beside
her, an older man fell into the most
prim and proper bride named Victoria.
He landed in her lap and his false
teeth skittered across the floor.
Sickened by the slimy sight, the upset
bride ran crying from the room. Nellie,
the mother hen, followed her.

The mayor elbowed through the men,
wiped sweat from his brow with the
handkerchief that he always carried and
begged the women to move apart.

Hannah and her chattering new
suitor found a spot across from the
door.

*This is good. I'll see Harland the
moment he comes in. I can head out the
back door before he spots me. I am the
only witness to what he did. He needs
me gone. He could have easily arrived
here from Boston by now.*

She tried to keep her mind on what
the clean-shaven suitor said, but she
found it difficult.

***

The door suddenly banged open,
profiled in the darkness outside the

doorway stood a tall, thin man standing behind an elderly, frail woman who had stepped into the light.

"He's found me," Hannah muttered, ready to bolt. Her heart pounded in her chest, and her ears rung with the blood rushing through her arteries. She flung her punch glass into her suitor's hand and gathered her skirts to run. The tall, thin shadow stepped into the light, and she realized her mistake.

Cage McCormack walked in behind the small, white haired lady. She recognized him as the man with the baritone voice that had almost run her down with his wagon. She released her skirts and clutched her chest, trying to slow her heart. She patted at the hair high on her head with the other hand, and then stopped.

What am I doing?

Hannah tried to ignore him, but something about Cage compelled her to give him a second glance. There was something so attractive about this man. Her heart seemed to overlook the fear her mind felt toward him.

He wasn't dressed for a party and hadn't shaved. He wore denim and a worn work shirt, definitely not in attire for a party. Perhaps he had a wife waiting at home.

After he said a few words to Nellie, he left. Disappointment hung over her the rest of the evening.

Now when her nervous glance rested on the door, she watched for two men.

Both were tall and thin with black hair and very dark, brooding eyes.

***

Cage stepped into the hall behind his mother.

"Good evenin, Cage. What brings you to the big reception?" Nellie straightened one of the streamers by the door.

"Evenin', Nellie. I brought Mama in. There was no way she was sittin' home while all this was goin' on."

"Are you gonna take time to meet some of the new ladies in town? I could introduce you."

"Naw." Cage rubbed at the two days of growth on his chin. "I was thinkin' I'd just hang out at the livery til Mama's ready to go home."

Cage's dark eyes rested on the small woman named Hannah.

"I'd be glad to introduce you. . ."

"No, no," Cage stated emphatically, placing his worn Stetson back in place.

"Get one of the men to come get me when Mama's ready, would you please, Nellie?"

"Sure, okay." Nellie smiled as the tall, thin rancher took his leave.

He took one last look at the bride in the pink dress. *The last time I saw her she had dirt all over that pretty mouth. A man would have a hard time to keep his mind off those lips.*

Chapter Three

Hannah's lips were on Cage's mind as he strolled to the livery stable. He knew a man such as him, not a devout Christian, would naturally hang out at the bar while he waited. But, he had no desire to be around rowdy old married men. Or single one's past their prime. He figured that's all that would be in the bar tonight with the big party at the town hall going on. No, he preferred spending time with his best friend Nikolai and the horses at the livery.

He found Nikolai finishing a pair of horseshoes at the forge. Sweat glistened on his large muscular frame. "Evenin' Cage, why aren't you at the hall chasin' women?"

Cage took a seat on a nearby barrel and watched as his friend pounded the iron into the proper shape on the anvil. "Well, I'm sure not here 'cause your company is any better." He waited to say more while the horseshoe sizzled in the cold water.

"I thought I would look after the place so you could go check out the brides. You're the one who wants to get married, not me."

"Do you mean it?" Nikolai said, his face animated.

Cage nodded and that was all it took. Nikolai untied the large protective leather apron he wore.

"Thanks, I'll get a bath and be back to get dressed."

Cage smiled, he had made his buddy happy. He picked up a currycomb and began brushing down the horses.

Nikolai came back and left for the reception. Cage, enjoying the solitude, worked his way to the stalls at the back, currying and talking to the horses as he went. He enjoyed spending time with God's creatures.

He was bent down examining the speckled gelding, Snowball's leg when he heard a noise near the door. The two silhouetted figures hadn't seen him because they were in the process of stealing old man Hansen's, palomino.

Outraged, Cage thought about how to stop the two men. They were in the stall close to the front door stumbling around drunkenly. It took two of them to saddle the shying horse. Cage crept around the shadows of the barn searching for a weapon. A pitchfork would have to do.

He slipped out the back door and dashed to the front hoping to stop them before they could mount the horse. His heart pounded as he ran. The Hansen boys were known as scrapers provoking fights when drunk. Clearly outnumbered he figured this would be a tough fight. But he wasn't about to let his friend down.

He faced the two men in the large open doorway of the livery. He felt silly facing them with just a pitchfork.

"Well, looky here, Hans. We got ourselves a problem." The big one noticed Cage first and alerted his brother.

Cage swallowed the painful lump in his throat and stood his ground as the two turned to face him.

"You boys just stop what you're doin' and leave and no one needs to get hurt." That even sounded lame to Cage's ears, but at least the fear he felt wasn't in his voice.

The two big farmers stumbled toward him laughing and sharing grins. "You plannin' on takin' both of us on, McCormack?" Hans sneered.

"If I have to," Cage said, wishing he could wipe the sweat off his brow. It was starting to run into his eyes and make them sting. He knew if he lost concentration they would be on him like fleas on a dog.

Seconds ticked by like hours as the three stood staring each other down. Cage worked the problem in his mind trying to think how he could end this without violence. Then it came to him, he backed off enough until the two had come out behind the palomino. Then he used the pitchfork to threaten them back against the horse's rump. Then the horse gave a mighty kick and the two went flying into the dirt at Cage's feet. Grinning widely Cage stuck both of the men with the tines of the fork. "Now, git."

When Nikolai came back from the hall, Cage was still laughing at the way the two men had skedaddled like two hounds with their tails between their legs.

***

Hannah, overwhelmed with all the constant chatter, and tension of continuously watching the door, began to tire and was glad when the evening wrapped up, Sheriff Campbell approached. "Miss Wall, may I walk you home?"

The barrel-chested sheriff with the sleek black hair made her feel safe, and he wasn't hard to look at either. She glanced up into his rugged face. "Certainly, sir."

Five of the other brides and their escorts joined Hannah and the sheriff for the three-block walk to their hotel. She felt comfortable in their company as she and Mitch followed the others at the end of the queue. As they passed the saloon, overwrought voices, embroiled in a heated argument, blasted through the door, Mitch hesitated and the others walked on without them.

"Miss Wall, I'm sorry. I should go in and see if I can calm things down in there."

"Certainly, I'll wait out here."

"I'll send someone you can trust to escort you home. All right?"

"Yes, go. I'll be fine," Hannah waved him on his way.

Her breath caught as his large bulk disappeared through the saloon doors. She took a seat on a nearby bench with her shawl clutched firmly around her shoulders her knees pressed tightly together. The smell of stale beer and a cloud of smoke came wafting out, and her nose wrinkled in disgust.

She made a quick survey of the dark shadows around her.

"I hope this doesn't take long," she muttered, as her teeth chattered, her body's unbidden reaction to being left alone. The other brides had reached the hotel in the distance, and their comforting chatter ceased.

Her eyes darted toward every sound. Leaves stirred in a nearby bush. A dog crossed the street his nails clicked on the boardwalk as he clipped along. She could hear but no longer see him.

The music stopped inside, then came the sound of a scuffle and angry male voices. Her head turned when she heard a large crash, the sound of furniture breaking, and then loud moaning.

Without thinking, she ran inside the bar to see who was hurt.

Several men milled around, their drinks still in their hands. The sheriff had a very drunk man bent over the bar, who loudly protested with some scathing, colorful language. Hannah knelt in the sawdust and examined an elderly man who had a large gash on his head. A walnut sized lump was already forming, and blood dripped through his beard toward the floor.

"Please, bring me a clean towel and some ice," she asked the bartender, over her shoulder.

Scott, the red-headed young man, hurried to comply. "Is there anything else I can do?" He leaned down to hand her the ice.

"Yes. Let's sit him up in a chair. Can you get the doctor? He's going to need stitches."

"Come on Charlie," Scott encouraged, hoisting the man with Hannah's help, "You need to see Doc."

"Oh, no, I don't," the grizzled old timer protested, twisting to get out of their grasp. "Ya ain't takin' me to no doc."

Hannah smiled to herself as Scott helped her get the old man up and seated on a nearby ladder-back chair. She'd had many patients like him before. Taught by Doc Jansen in Boston she had spent many hours in people's homes nursing them back to health. Mitch had one of the beer-swilling bar patrons go for the doctor. The others stood around drinking the last of their drinks enjoying the excitement.

"You all right, Miss Wall?" Mitch asked from the bar. "You shouldn't be in here."

Their eyes met across the smoky expanse and Hannah watched as the situation dawned on Mitch's handsome face.

"You've done this before."

She smiled and their eyes lingered.

As they waited for Doc to arrive, Hannah held a bar towel to the old timer's head putting pressure on the wound. With her other hand, she brushed at the debris still on her skirt. Her best dress was ruined with spittle and spilled beer from the floor.

When everything had settled down, the sheriff arranged for Scott to escort her back to the hotel. The injured man would be fine, though he would proudly be sporting Doc's stitches as a badge of honor tomorrow. And the drunken furniture thrower would spend the night in jail.

As Hannah prepared for bed later that night, she prayed for Charlie, Scott and the others she had met that day. Her last thought as she drifted off was of Cage McCormack. Strange how her mind dwelled on the one brief second of tenderness and concern, he showed her. It unexplainably drew her thoughts to him. She finished her prayers and settled deeper into her quilts while Bernice snored softly beside her.

***

Mitch walked the town doing his rounds.

She's a tiny thing. Brave though, to come charging in where she shouldn't be. She sure took charge of the situation and knew just what to do. No other women he knew could have done it. His insides tightened as he thought of a woman like her by his side. I'd love her to be my bride. If he wanted Hannah, he had better make a plan to win her before someone else jumped ahead of him.

He checked the livery. Nikolai, the big blacksmith, startled him with his snoring as he passed the open door of the tack room. Mitch slipped in and out so as not to wake him. All was quiet in town until he neared the hotel again. He came down the back alley and heard angry female voices. They came through a window he knew led to the second floor hallway. He slipped up the dark back stairway to see what was going on. Two of the brides stood in the doorway of one of the rooms. The one with the upper hand had the shorter blonde backed up against the door jam. She was almost spitting in the other women's face she was so agitated. Her brown hair, tied in rags to curl her hair while she slept, bounced as she flung words at her adversary.

"Ladies, ladies," he called softly, "keep your voices down. What seems to be the problem here?"

"She takes all the covers, and I keep waking up cold."

"She won't let me sleep," the other one sniveled, near tears. Rag doll shoved Sleepy and Mitch stepped between them before this cat fight could get ugly. While Sleepy cowered on the far side of the hall, Mitch had his hands full restraining Rag Doll who was now showering him with colorful language for stepping in.

Nellie, the hotel owner, appeared at the end of the hall, blurry-eyed and annoyed.

"You got a room ya can move one of these ladies to?"

"Well, yes," she admitted, as she finished tying the belt on her wrapper.

"Good." He turned to Rag Doll and commanded, "Get your stuff and go with her."

He waited while Nellie settled them and wished he had encountered Hannah. It would have been pleasant to see her in the hall in her nightgown instead of the blonde-haired woman.

"Some days, this job tries a body's patience," he muttered as he headed to the jail, disappointed that Hannah must have slept through the skirmish.

Mitch finished his rounds, and finding everything peaceful and his prisoner sound asleep, he retired for the night to his quarters beside the jail.

As he lay in his big lonely bed, under the quilt that Grandma Campbell had made him, his last thoughts were of Hannah.

I wonder if she would like sharing my life as a sheriff's wife.

***

Cage received word that his mother was ready to go home. He walked from the livery stable back to the Town Hall. As he entered the wooden structure, he noticed the noise level was much lower now. The hall itself had changed in appearance too. Many of the streamers carefully placed earlier had let go and hung down some littering the floor. The neatly arranged chairs were now in clusters as if several queens had held court with their subjects in attendance around them. Most of the people had gone too.

He found his mother near the door and he helped her put on her well-worn wool coat.

"How was it, Mama? Did you have a good time?"

"Yes, Micajah dear, thank you for bringing me. I've lots to tell you on the way home."

Cage said nothing as he took his mother's arm. He noticed she had become less steady on her feet over the past year.

His eyes swept the room for the bride in the pink dress with the auburn hair, and he lost interest when he didn't find her. He didn't want to admit it to himself, but he was disappointed when she wasn't there. He felt like the Christmas when he had come to the tree only to find one small pitiful package. He wasn't about to confess that the whole time he spent with the horses, Hannah had been very much in his mind. When would he see her again?

"Come, Mama, let's get you home. We don't want you getting ill."

Chapter Four

Cage awoke to the sound of Frederick, Mama's old rooster, and went out to check on things in the yard and the barn. Mama fussed in the kitchen getting breakfast. When he came back to the house, he found her lying in a heap. He ran to help her up and noticed her mouth drooped, and her words slurred strangely.

"Mama, Mama, you all right?"

She tried to answer, but her speech came out garbled. He hooked under her arms and lifted but she slumped, her right leg gave out under her weight.

That's when panic rose in him, taking an icy grip on his heart. He grabbed a sweater that hung on the back of a nearby chair and pillowed her head.

"Lay still Mama. I'll be right back." He ran to hitch up the wagon.

I'll get her to Doc's. She'll be fine. Doc'll fix her.

He hitched the wagon with shaking hands. He had trouble working the buckles, and the horse that always stood quiet, wouldn't stand still.

He raced back to the house. She sat on the floor and held on to a wooden kitchen chair leg like a drowning man holds on to the last piece of floating debris from a sinking ship.

His chest tightened, and his hands clenched at the way she looked up at him with bewildered eyes. She reached out to him and tried to say something, but her speech ran together, and he couldn't understand.

"It's all right, Mama. Just a minute," he tried to reassure her, as he ran to get a quilt. He wrapped her in it. Hugging her in his arms tightly, he carried her to the waiting wagon.

"I'm takin' ya to Doc's."

He placed her first on the seat beside him, but with one weak side, she almost toppled off.

Something is very wrong.

He bundled her into the bed of the wagon. The sound of her soft cries tore at his heart.

Tears stung his eyes as he slapped the horse's rump, and the wagon lurched forward.

Terrified, Cage whipped the horses harder. Something real bad was wrong with Mama, and he had to get her to Doc's. Nothing else in this world mattered more than her and something was not right. He looked over his shoulder at the pitifully small bundle.

"You'll be fine. I'll get you to town, Mama."

The awakening prairie flew past while he whipped the horses as hard as he dared. Clouds, tinged with pink, scudded across the horizon, and he hollered urging the horses faster along the wheel tracks. Prairie hens rose out of the grass, but he paid them no mind.

Mama gave a soft moan from the wagon bed. Fear left a bitter taste in Cage's mouth as he willed the miles to pass.

They finally thundered up to Doc's door. Cage wiped a tear away, before he could lift his mother out of the back of the wagon. Cage kicked at the door until Doc answered.

"Somethin's wrong with Mama." Cage rushed to set his mother down so Doc could examine her.

After his first look at Cage's mother, the worry lines in Doc's brow frightened Cage. "This looks like a stroke, boy."

"Is she gonna be all right?"

"I can't rightly tell just yet." The doctor continued his examination. "How long she been talkin' like this?"

"Since I found her not long ago," Cage told him, unable to keep the worry from his voice.

"See how she has no strength or control on this one side?"

"Yeah."

"Well, that's for sure a stroke."

"Will she get better, Doc?" Cage had visions of her being a cripple.

"I won't be able ta tell for a few days. You best leave her here, with the missus and me, 'til we see how she's gonna recover."

Cage looked down into his mother's frightened face and gave her a reassuring smile.

"You all right with that, Mama? I'll be back every day."

She nodded, her eyes like round saucers.

"Don't you worry, Mama. Doc and his missus will take good care of yah. And I'll get you home, as soon as he says you're all better."

Doc walked Cage to the door and whispered to him, "You best get someone to take care of her when you get her home."

"I can look after her."

"That's commendable, but she can't even dress herself or use the privy without help, son."

"Who am I gonna get, Doc?" A feeling, like the one when he fell out of the tree the year he turned seven, gripped him.

"One of the new brides has some nursin'. She helped patch up ole Charlie Weeks. You need to be askin' her."

"Which one would that be?"

"Hannah, the short, purity one."

***

Cage found Hannah at the hotel. She sat with several of the brides enjoying mid-afternoon tea in the fireside room. For a moment, he stood in the doorway, watching her pretty oval face in animated conversation. A small curl had escaped and hung down, just kissing her shoulder next to her collar. Strange how something so simple could cause a peculiar turning in his gut.

He shook his head, hoping to clear it of such nonsense, and stepped into the room. The red-haired bride noticed him first and acknowledged him in her nasal voice.

"Well, hello. Come and join us, sir."

Uncomfortable in a room full of women, like a long tail cat in a room full of rockers, he said, "I need to speak to Hannah for a moment."

Hannah stood from her chair by the unlit fireplace and set her teacup on a nearby coffee table.

"I'm Hannah."

"Could we step into the dining room for a moment?" He squeezed his hat in his hands, distorting the brim.

"Yes, of course." She bit her lip, and Cage realized she was worried. As the two of them left the room several brides twittered.

Eager to allay her fears, he looked her in the eye. "I need to talk to you about my Mama. She's suffered a stroke, and I understand from Doc that you know some nursin'."

"Yes, I do, but I had not thought of using it while I'm here."

"Miss, I wish you would consider comin' to my farm and helping me take care of my mother. Doc tells me she is gonna need help with the simplest of tasks, like dressin' and bathin', things that I can't do for her."

His eyes traced her, surveyed her face as she thought through his proposal. He watched for a sign that she would agree to his plan. He shifted listlessly as he waited, wondering what he would do if she refused. His hands had begun to sweat onto the brim of his hat.

"You wouldn't be proposing marriage, would you?"

"No, no, just nursing, Miss. Just- nursing. Ah, carin' for Mama." That gave him a terrible fright. His heart was still hammering. What made her think he wanted to get married?

"When would you need me to start?" Her face had reddened too.

"In a day or two. I can't pay you much, but your room and food would be taken care of until Mama can care for herself again."

He could see her hesitation and wondered what he should say to convince her. "I could help sometimes with some of the chores," he blurted, then thought better of it.

    I hope I don't come to regret that last remark.

Chapter Five

Hannah stared up into the tall man's frightening dark face. Cage, with his uncanny resemblance to Harland, made her want to run from him. His black eyes held no warmth. The smell of cow dung on his clothes made her nose wrinkle.

Hiding out of town at his ranch might be a good thing. Harland wouldn't find me there.

She wrung her hands as indecision weighed like a mantle on her shoulders. She watched him shift listlessly and pin her with his eyes, waiting for an answer. He looked desperate.

She was afraid of him and he smelled bad. How could she live with him? Then she thought of his mother, the sweet lady he'd escorted into the town hall. She needed the kind of care that Hannah could provide. How could she refuse?

"All right, Mr. McCormack. I'll take care of your mother."

Relief, like an ocean tide, flooded his solemn face, and he shook her hand like he was pumping for water at the well. For the tiniest of seconds, she saw warmth in his stormy, black eyes. Then it disappeared, and he was all business.

"I'll send word to you when Doc says Mama can come home."

"Yes, all right." She took a step back where the cattle odor couldn't reach her. "I'll speak to the doctor and find out what care your mother will need, that way I'll be ready to come when she's able to travel."

"Thank you, Miss Wall."

"You're welcome, Mr. McCormack." Her eyes lingered on the thin, tall rancher as he donned his hat and walked out the door.

Hannah returned to the fireside room. The expectant face of every bride turned to greet her.

With arms crossed tightly on her chest, she announced, "I'll be moving to the McCormack ranch to care for Mrs. McCormack who has suffered apoplexy."

The room erupted in a cacophony of female voices, all asking questions at once.

***

Cage found Nellie in the kitchen baking cookies. She turned and straightened, dusting flour off her hands onto her apron.

"Well, hello, Cage. How is your mother?"

"I guess you heard she's feelin' poorly."

"Yes, is she any better?"

"About the same. I need to ask you if you happen to have a spare bed in storage. A single would do. Miss Hannah has agreed to come to the ranch and care for Mama. I have to move to the porch for the summer."

"Miss Hannah?" she asked with a raised brow. "Out back in the shed, let's see if what I got will be suitable," she said, leading the way to the back hall. "Miss Hannah is a right nice young lady," Nellie said.

"Yes, ma'am." Just the mention of her name made his face hot.

Cage found what he wanted, a simple single bed with a brass frame. He had Nikolai, the blacksmith, help him load it into his wagon. Nellie refused to take money for it.

"Just bring the bed back when you're finished with it."

***

Later that evening, he worked in his small bedroom trying to get ready for Hannah. Cage emptied his dresser and closet and moved his sheets and covers to the borrowed bed on the porch. He found fresh linens and tried to make up the bed.

He missed his mother's domestic skills as he stuggled with the mess he had made of the covers. It was off kilter. He couldn't seem to fix it to Mama's neat standard.

He shrugged and covered the jumble with an old quilt Grandma McCormack made. The coverlet had flower shapes sewn to the top of it. They seemed like red roses on leafy stems. He remembered how warm it was to cuddle under it as a kid on a cold winter's night. Mama had a way of tucking the quilt up neat under the pillow, but when he tried, it didn't look as nice.

Next, he straightened the kitchen as best he could, trying to see the room through a woman's eyes.

Don't want to discourage the poor girl the minute she walks in.

He put away things that had been left out during his mad scramble to get Mama to town and the mess that had accumulated in the meantime. Mama always kept a neat house.

A vision of Hannah in her pink party dress flashed through his memory. *She sure is a purty little filly.* A longing to have her at the stove cooking for him and looking after his mama overtook him. He needed to remember she would be here to look after his mother.

***

Hannah came in from her morning stroll and Nellie handed her a note.

"Not bad news I hope," concern peppered Nellie's voice.

"No. Mrs. McCormack will be ready to go home tomorrow."

"You'll have your hands full, dear."

"Yes, I expect so," she said, giving a weak smile.

"Will you need help to pack?"

"No, I've expected this and I'm sure Bernice will help with the final few things."

As she thought, Bernice helped her get her belongings together. "I'm going to miss you, Hannah."

Not wishing to be rude, she said, "It will be strange without you, too."

Hannah gave her hair one last pat and endured Bernice's third hug, then went to wait for Cage on the porch.

She said her goodbyes to Nellie and the others the night before.

Butterflies chased one another in her stomach as she sat biting her nails and rocking in the white wicker rocker.

Cage made her feel uncomfortable, but when she thought about how easy it would be for Harland to find her here in town, the country and Cage sounded like a better plan.

Soon, I'll be safe at the McCormack ranch.

Cage pulled up with his wagon and jumped down.

She gathered her reticule; the butterflies had flown to her chest now.

"You ready?"

"Yes." She tried a smile, with no response from him.

He roughly helped her climb up to the buckboard's high seat. She was certain there would be a bruise where he gripped her arm too tightly.

While Cage went to get her belongings, she grumbled to herself, "That man is so good to his mother, but look how he treats me. I wonder if he realizes how forceful and rude he is to me?"

Cage came back struggling with Hannah's many bags. He placed them in the rear of the wagon, muttering something she couldn't quite make out.

The wagon was a far cry from Doc's buggy. Hannah held tight to the hard wooden seat as they bounced and rocked over the ruts in the street.

It seemed to Hannah like Cage had taken the roughest route to get there. They bounced so hard into a pothole that she flew up almost losing her perch and he put his arm around her to prevent her falling. Tucked up close to him for that brief moment she smelled soap and sandalwood.

He had spruced up to come to town.

The scent made her want to stay where she was even though she could feel heat flushing her face.

He looked down at her briefly, one side of his mouth quirked in a suppressed grin. He patted her shoulder and took up the reins in both hands again.

They arrived at Doc's to pick up Cage's mother. Hannah went in with him, and Doc introduced the two women.

Hannah smiled warmly. "I'm pleased to meet you, ma'am."

Mrs. McCormack's friendly eyes took her in as they shook hands.

While Cage thanked Doc and went to settle his mama in the wagon, Doc spoke to Hannah, handing her a sheet of written instructions.

When Doc handed her the paper he said, "Mrs. McCormack has recovered more of her ability to speak, but her right side is still very weak."

Hannah had a sinking feeling as she answered, "She'll need help to dress and bathe for a long time to come."

Doc only nodded. "I'll try to get by and check in once a week when I'm makin' my rounds. Send Cage right away or bring her in if there's a relapse." Doc smiled and escorted her to the door. "I'm sure you'll do just fine."

"I'll certainly do my best. Thanks, Doc."

Cage helped Hannah up onto the wagon's bench-seat beside his mother.

Mrs. McCormack flashed her a friendly smile and Hannah had no regrets about the decision she made to work for her. She could only hope all would go well when they reached the farm.

Chapter Six

The trip by wagon seemed endless to Hannah. In Boston, a carriage ride took perhaps half an hour at most. Here, they bumped along well-worn ruts for three times as long. She became uncomfortable a short time into the journey; not only her bones ached, but muscles she had never used before were now constantly needed to hold her onto the bouncing seat. She frequently needed to adjust and compensate. She worried about how Mrs. McCormack must be feeling and tried to brace her with an arm around the frail woman's midsection.

"Is it much further?" Hannah asked.

She adjusted the pin in her hat in an effort to prevent it from flying off into the dusty road.

"No, dear, perhaps ten minutes. Right, Micajah?" Mrs. McCormack answered, in a slightly slurred manner.

"Not long now, miss." His baritone voice quivered as they hit washboard ruts in the road. He flashed her a dark look. She was sorry if her presence was an inconvenience to this man.

Eventually, they reached the farmyard, and a black and white border collie rushed out to greet them. He barked and ran circles around the wagon as they pulled up to the back door. Hannah watched him warily and wondered if he was friendly.

Hannah took a moment to take in her surroundings. The farmhouse was small, sided with white clapboard. The barn loomed three times the size of the house and stood several yards behind it. Three spotted horses grazed in a corral beside the rustic building. A water pump stood between the two buildings, a long walk to get water.

A few poplar trees grew in the yard, but still too small to offer much shade. The outer perimeter of the very large two acre yard was planted with caragana bushes to provide a windbreak. And from there, the prairie stretched flat grassland for endless miles to the horizon.

Cage jumped down and offered her his hand. She gathered her skirt and with her reticule clasped firmly she put her small soft hand into his callused one. Her feet touched the ground and her legs were too shaky to hold her. She teetered momentarily then fell into his arms. When she gained her balance and could stand, she met his wide surprised dark fringed eyes. Her heart fluttered and she felt a flush stain her cheeks. She still had a death grip on his forearms, and she watched his eyes travel to them. Embarrassed, she let go.

"Sorry," she mumbled, lowering her eyes.

She turned her attention to helping him get his mother down and safely tucked into a chair in the living room. The dog ran up, his tail wagging in friendly greeting as he trotted after them. Hannah steered away from him and was glad he kept his distance.

"Please don't fuss, dear." Mrs. McCormack waved her off as Hannah tried to make her comfortable. She pulled a foot stool over and tucked an afghan over her.

"Get a fire started in the stove," Cage barked from the door. "Out," he commanded the black and white dog, as he left to go out to the wagon.

Aching from the rough ride from town, Hannah wished she could sit for a moment and get her bearings. She forced herself to the stove, found matches and lit a fire. The smell of wood smoke soon filled the kitchen, and she searched until she found what she needed to serve tea.

Cage brought in her bags. "The room upstairs is yours."

"Thank you." She shivered, as the annoyed look he gave her was so much like the ones Harland gave her when he had to do her a favor.

She walked out into the screened-in front porch while she waited for her water to boil. Cage's mother dozed in her chair as Hannah passed through the living room. She noticed an ill-made bed at one end. A homey sitting area with a well-worn settee sat at the opposite end. A leafy plant stood in one corner and several small pots of baby plants lined the window ledge. Sunlight streamed through the many windows and made the porch homey and pleasant, an ideal spot to bring a book and read.

Hannah stood for a brief moment looking out the bank of windows down the long rutted lane toward town. The black and white dog romped in the grass along the laneway.

She would be able to see Harland coming from here. Hannah frowned. And then what would she do?

Hopefully, Cage would be nearby. Would he be any protection if Harland meant her harm? Would the taciturn man even care?

"Please, may this be a safe harbor, Lord," she prayed.

The teakettle whistled and called her from her musing. She readied a cup of tea for herself, Cage and his mother with some cookies from the pantry. Hannah placed them on the kitchen table

where some neglected wildflowers hung their heads from a small glass vase.
Had Cage picked them for his mother? What a nice gesture.
She helped Mrs. McCormack to the table and Cage came downstairs to join them.
"Is this all you're servin'?"
Taken aback she snapped, "Would you like your evening meal now?"
"No, but a body needs more than this after such a long ride."
Her eyes flew to Cage's mother and the older lady suggested, "There's beef jerky in the pantry, dear." Smiling at him, she added, "Will that fill the gap?"
He drank the rest of his tea in one gulp and got up, scraping his chair across the hardwood. "Forget it." And with that he went to the back door, a handful of cookies in hand. He grabbed his jacket and left.
Hannah sat stunned. She wasn't used to people acting so temperamental.
"Sorry dear, I'll speak to him," Mrs. McCormack said in her slurred speech, looking embarrassed.
Concerned for her patient, Hannah bundled her off to her bedroom next to the living room. As Hannah tucked the weary woman under a wedding ring quilt, she asked, "What shall I prepare for supper?"
In her slurred way of talking, Mrs. McCormack answered, "There is leftover

ham in the cellar, or you can kill a chicken if you like, dear."

The idea of killing an animal made her think she might easily lose the few cookies she had just eaten. Hannah turned quickly and left the room knowing her disgust must clearly show on her face.

Maybe this hiding out on a farm wasn't such a good idea.

It took her a few minutes, but she discovered the door to the cellar on the outside of the house. When Hannah went in the dank room under the building, she wished she had thought to bring a candle or lantern with her. Watching for spiders and creepy things, her skin crawled as she tried to hurry and find the correct crock in the dimly lit space. Closing the door with the right ceramic jar in hand, she gave an involuntary shiver.

Who knew what was lurking in the shadows of the little room?

In Boston, most people had ice boxes. The cold cellar seemed primitive, and she grumbled as she made her way back to the kitchen. She let out a gasp when she opened the back door. Mrs. McCormack sat at the table peeling potatoes.

"How are you feeling now, Mrs. McCormack?"

"Fit as a fiddle now, dear."

"Please, let me do that," Hannah said, trying to take the knife from her.

"I'm not broken. I can do this."

Hannah smiled to herself at the feisty little woman.

With her impaired hand, the peels were chunky and uneven, but Hannah was not about to argue.

"You need to milk the cow, dear."

"Pardon?"

"Bessy will be waiting at the barn door now. You'll find the pail and the stool at the south end of the building."

I have never been near a cow in my life. Does this lady really think I can do this? I can't even stand the smell of them. Let alone get near enough to touch their private parts.

"Won't Cage be milking the cow?" she tried in a hopeful voice.

"Oh no, dear, Micajah has many others things he will be busy doing."

For a second, she thought about asking Mrs. McCormack to milk the cow, and then realized that was just not an option. She was desperate, but not that desperate.

She put her jacket on and went to see if she could find Cage and talk him into milking the cow. The prairie wind whipped at her skirt as she crossed the yard.

She was supposed to be here to look after a patient. Instead, she was doing everything but. That overgrown man had her at his beck and call wanting her to kill chickens and milk cows and who knew what next? Rounding up cows or what ever they did with them. And he better not expect her to go down into the hole under the house again. Who knew what bug would jump on her under there? Why didn't they have an ice box like normal people? Taking advantage is what he was doing. She had only been here a couple of hours, and she was all ready beginning to regret her decision.

Chapter Seven

Hannah walked into the dimly lit, cavernous barn and heard a cow in distress. The odor of dung and animal, assailed her and she pinched her nose. She followed the sound of Cage's baritone voice as he gently talked in a soothing manner to a laboring cow whose bawling echoed off the walls.

As she tiptoed up to the stall, her vision adjusted to the dim daylight in the building. The cow was lying on her side breathing heavily and tossing her head. From the rear of the cow, kneeling in the straw, Cage turned to her, "Calf is comin' early," he whispered. "Get up by her head and talk to her."

Hannah blinked dumbfounded down at this tall stranger who had just asked the impossible of her.

She tried changing the subject. "Will you please milk the cow, for your mother?"

He froze and slowly turned his head to stare at her. "Can't you see I'm busy?"

She wavered uncertain, wondering what she should do.

He wanted her to kneel down in that dirty straw with mouse droppings and who knew what else in it. And his mother wanted her to milk the cow by touching its private parts. This is not what she was hired for. She stood undecided. She wanted to either run or cry.

The cow was clearly in anguish now; she kicked and swung her head. Her bawling echoed through the building. "Are you gonna help?" Cage barked.

Tears of distress filled her eyes as she dropped to her knees beside the poor cow. She gingerly touched its warm, soft neck. She had no desire to be in this situation. She looked after humans not animals this was beyond her feeling of comfort. Yes, she felt sorry for the animal, but she did not want to be the one to help birth her calf.

"Talk to her. Your voice'll soothe her."

"Nice cow, nice cow."

Cage guffawed loudly.

"Her name is Bessy."

"Okay, Bessy, nice cow."

"This man expects a lot from someone who has never been in a barn before," she huffed under her breath.

The cow kicked and raised her head as if to get up.

"Hold her down, cord's around the neck."

She had no idea what that meant. Doc had never allowed her to help in birthing. He had considered her too young, but by the distress in Cage's voice, she knew it was serious. She did as he instructed, tears stinging the back of her eyes. This huge animal frightened her, it smelled really bad, and she just had no desire to be doing this. Her hands shook as she held the big head down. A large brown eye stared up at her. The cow's sides expanded with her breathing and her body jerked with the effort to expel the calf.

After several minutes, there was a sigh of relief from Cage and then she heard the calf struggle for its first breath.

"He's gonna be all right," he whispered.

After taking off the now slimy cotton gloves he wore, Cage rose and grabbed her hand and hauled her to her feet. "She knows what to do from here."

Cage pulled Hannah to him and wrapped his arm securely around her shoulders holding her out of harm's way. His warmth radiated from him, and she didn't move away as would be proper. They stood mesmerized as the cow cleaned the calf. Hannah was in awe of the miracle she had just witnessed. Maternal instincts stirred deep within making her smile. She realized that instead of being intimated by the strength of his hold, she liked being tucked under Cage's shoulder, safe and warm. They stood a moment longer in companionable silence watching the cow with her baby.

"I'll milk Bessy tonight. Go see to Mama's supper," he said, giving her a push on the back.

Cage's gentleness and concern for the animals impressed her as she walked back through the moonlit yard.

Could he be a God fearing man and be so compassionate at times and harbor so much anger too?

***

Cage sat on the stool milking Bessy and wondered if bringing a city girl to the farm was a good idea. Yet, he needed her help; he couldn't run the entire farm by himself. It seemed everything made her jumpy. She'd even shied away from his dog. Well, she was just going to have to adjust.

As the pail filled with milk, he thought about how she had looked when the calf came sliding out into the straw. She was beautiful in the dim light with such an expression of awe in her bright eyes. Tendrils of her auburn hair had come loose and cascaded to frame her perfect face.

When he thought of it now, a longing came over him, a desire for her to like it here on the ranch with him and Mama.

He got up and shook his head to rid himself of such silly thinking. No girl as nice as Hannah would ever want him. He was dirt poor and full of anger.

He stopped at the pump to wash up on the way to supper. Darkness was falling and birds called to one another from the trees. He would come back later to check on the calf, but for now two sweet women waited for him in the house.

The warmth of the kitchen and the aroma of freshly cooked vegetables met him when he entered. Mama sat at her usual spot at the table; she appeared worn and tired in the lamp light. He made a mental note to get her off to bed as soon as they finished supper.

Hannah bustled at the stove. "We havin' company?" he asked, when he sat down and noticed the table set with the fine china.

Mama gave him a look, and he backed down. "It's a special occasion," she told him, defending Hannah's choice of tableware. "We bein' tagether for the first time and all."

Hannah brought the plates of savory stew and fresh bread to the table, and sat down. Cage tied into his.

Mama cleared her throat, and he glanced up to realize by the look on Hannah's face that she had expected them to say grace.

He swallowed the large mouthful of potatoes and almost choked. Then dutifully, he bowed his head waiting for his mother or Hannah to have their say, so he could get on with his meal.

The silence drifted on until Hannah's voice broke the silence. "Cage, will you please say the grace?"

His eyes flew open, and he could see from her bowed head that she was dead serious. He had never said grace in his life. Well, since he was a little shaver. His mother caught his eye and gave him a look that said behave yourself.

Yes, Mama, he answered in his head. Now what to say?

"Thanks Lord, for this here food and for the fine ladies that prepared it, amen," he said, heat flooding his unhappy face.

He kept his head down not wanting to see the women's reaction to that poor excuse of a grace. Once again, he dug into his meal somber now, but thoroughly enjoying it.

When it came time for dessert, Cage watched as Hannah dished peach preserves into small glass bowls. The portion she gave him wasn't near enough. In three spoonfuls, it was gone.

"Can I get seconds?"

"I can get more from the cellar," she offered.

He pinned her with a disgusted look.

"Forget it," he told her scraping his chair across the floor in his haste to leave. He left her gaping as he went to check on his new calf. "A man could go hungry," he griped under his breath.

***

Hannah's first concern was to get Mrs. McCormack settled in bed. After a trip to the privy and a good wash, Hannah helped the older woman with her nightgown and plaited her long gray hair. When she was all tucked into bed, Hannah said goodnight and took the lamp with her into the kitchen.

She cleared the table and was doing the dishes when Cage came in.

"How is the new calf?" she asked, as he stoked the fire in the stove for the night.

"He's doin' fine. Up taking nourishment."

"Good." She met his dark gaze over her shoulder. As she turned back to the dishes, she wondered what went on behind those dark unfathomable eyes.

Cage cleared his throat, "Good night, miss."

Without waiting for a reply, he went to the front porch and closed the door. She had seen the ill-made bed there earlier and guessed that was where he would spend the night.

She finished tidying the kitchen and took the lamp to use the privy, out behind the house. She stood at the back door with the lamp held high surveying the yard. Her first thought was: Boston was never like this.

A shiver went up her spine as she hiked up her skirt and started in the direction of the outhouse. The sound of cattle calling reached her from the surrounding darkness. A hundred stars held their place in the heavens and a half-moon helped light her way. She reached the rough-hewn boards of the privy and struggled with the latch. As her fear of all bugs overwhelmed her, she watched for dreaded spiders and hurriedly did her business, holding her breath until she could leave the smelly, little building.

On the way back, she heard a coyote howl. She yelped and ran for the safety of the house. Her heart pounded as she slammed the back door on the prairie night.

Coyotes can't get in here, can they?

To make sure, she propped a chair against both doors. She tiptoed into her patient's room. The small outline in the bed rose and fell in a steady rhythm.

Exhaustion weighed on her as she climbed the stairs to Cage's former room. She spent time in prayer and drifted off to sleep wondering why Cage had so much anger bottled up inside. *Help me discover the source of all that*

. . . misdirected . . . anger . . . Lord.
 Then she drifted in thought until sleep claimed her.

Chapter Eight

Cage awoke the next morning to Frederick, Mama's old rooster, crowing as proud and loud as possible. Cage needed to use the privy. He started to go out the front door and found it cold outside. He'd left his jacket at the back door, so he decided to go through the house to get it. He took hold of the inner door and pushed to go through. His forehead hit the door and rattled his teeth while pain shot into his skull.

What? It was jammed. Well, how would that happen?

He rubbed the knot forming on his head and tried it again, and no, it wouldn't budge.

He bounced from foot to foot now, the urge to get to the privy even greater. He ran out the front door without his coat or his shoes knowing he would be cold in the fresh spring air. The stones in the yard bit into his feet as he hurried to the back of the house. Bear met him about halfway and barked, running circles around him, trying to herd him. But Cage would have none of that and made a beeline to the outhouse.

The door hung open. Strange. They always kept the door shut. When he got close enough to peer inside, he spotted a black and white cat sleeping in a dark corner where the light hadn't disturbed it. Oh no.

Unfortunately, Bear had noticed it now and began to bark in a frenzy. Cage grabbed for the fur on the dog's neck to pull him back but Bear was too intent on his quarry.

"No, Bear, no!" He pulled hard. "Come Bear, come."

Any other time Bear was good to obey, but not today.

Too late.

The air filled with the noxious odor of a full-blown skunk attack. The two black and white animals, one dog, one skunk, streaked across the yard, scattering horses as they ran through the corral. Cage coughed and choked on the fumes and wrinkled his nose in disgust.

The urge to use the privy was now a burning need. There was no way he was going in the outhouse with the potent reek of skunk filling the small space. Cage, couldn't wait any longer, and stepped behind the privy where a huge patch of grass became wet as relief flooded him.

He walked back to the house and wondered who had left the outhouse open. It must have happened when Hannah made her final trip last night. He would have to talk to her about the consequences of not latching the door tight.

He shivered from the cold and his bare feet had mud on them from the dew in the grass.

He reached the back door, hoping the skunk odor in the air hadn't penetrated his clothes. Maybe, what he smelled was drifting from the privy. He rattled the door and kicked at it but couldn't get in.

What is going on here?

"Hannah." Angry as a bear woken up in spring, he shook the door again.

He heard shuffling and scraping wood then his mother peeked out the door. He brushed past her in his anger.

He held back a grin when he noticed Hannah's home made lock. A ladder-back chair sat by the door. Hannah had been frightened and locked herself in. He shook his head and rubbed his jaw. Again, he wondered if a city girl in the country was a good idea.

***

Hannah woke to the sound of pans clattering downstairs.

She sat bolt upright. *Oh my, I've slept in!*

She pulled her nightgown off over her head and shivered in the predawn chill. Scrambling for clothes and under things, she hurried to dress. Cage would be angry, but there was nothing she could do about it.

In her haste nothing went right, her stockings twisted and wouldn't straighten until she pulled them off and tried again. When she pulled the bloomers on, there was a strange bulge in the front. Oh goodness, she had them on backwards.

Her heart raced as she clacked down the stairs in her high-button shoes. No time to buttonhook them and the leather flapped against her ankles.

She took the ribbon she had carried in her teeth out of her mouth and stood at the bottom of the stairs scooping her hair back from her face. The tie made a tiny ponytail that would look childish, but she was late, she had no choice.

She rounded the corner into the kitchen to find Cage measuring oatmeal into a large pot of boiling water. The coffee bubbled sending a delicious aroma throughout the room. Embarrassment heated her face.

"Please let me do that."

"Mama's waiting for you." A stern tone in his voice, Cage sent a frosty look over his shoulder.

"I'm here, dear. Could you help me to the privy?" Mrs. McCormack spoke from the doorway.

"Of course. I'm sorry." Hannah turned and helped her put on a soft woolen shawl.

As they walked to the back, she tried to apologize.

"I'm so sorry, Mrs. McCormack. We must find a way that you can call me when I'm needed."

"No harm done, dear. But yes, a bell would work nicely. If we ask Micajah, he may have a cowbell we can use."

They made their way to the convenience. Hannah watched carefully for anything that might cause her patient to turn an ankle. The black and white dog ran circles around them happily wagging his tail.

She waited for Mrs. McCormack while the old woman used the outhouse. They both had to plug their nose to avoid the retched smell. Hannah shivered as large billowing clouds shifted patterns in the dawn sky over the prairie. She wished now she had brought her buttonhook with her. She could have used this time to get her shoes properly hooked. The flapping on her ankles had become annoying.

She remembered now hearing the rooster crow, but she must have fallen back asleep.

As they walked to the house together, Hannah thought about the anger she would face when they entered the kitchen again. Would he stay silent or rave at her? With what little she knew of the man, she thought he would glare at her with those scary dark eyes of his and say nothing.

The warmth in the room was welcome as she helped Mrs. McCormack take off her shawl and settled her into a seat at the table. Her heart sped up as Cage spooned brown sugar onto his lumpy oatmeal. His rugged stubbled face held a scowl. Her tardiness had put it there. Their eyes met. He looked her up and down, but said not a word. Regret hit her.

Just as she was serving Mrs. McCormack her porridge and coffee, and wondering when Cage would reprimand her, a racket erupted in the yard. The black and white collie greeted someone with a long flurry of welcoming barks.

"What's got Bear so excited?" asked Mrs. McCormack.

Cage went to the back door, "Carter Henderson and a red-haired woman just pulled up. I've work to do."

Hannah rolled her eyes as soon as she heard the woman's voice. It had to be Bernice. She wished now she had taken more time with her appearance. She didn't want Bernice going back and telling the others that she went around with her shoes undone and her hair in a childish hairstyle.

Bernice came and introduced the gap-toothed man with her. "Hannah this is Carter Henderson. He is the agent at the railway station in town."

The thin boney man had a strong grip.

"Bernice this is Cage McCormack and his mother."

Bernice came right in. "Mrs. McCormack how are you feeling now?"

Cage spoke briefly to Carter at the door, then left.

Not waiting for a reply, Bernice waved her arm. "We can't stay long." Then lightly touched Hannah's arm. "I've come with an invitation."

"Well please, sit and have coffee before you go back."

When Bernice had her coffee she took a sip then starred up at Hannah with a serious look. "The brides are having a cook-off in town. Carter has agreed to pick you up tomorrow and bring you to town. Each bride was to draw a potential groom's name from a hat, you weren't there so we drew for you and then you will prepare a meal for him in the hotel's kitchen. You'll share the meal alone in the dining room, and the groom will let the others know if you are a good cook."

"I could make beef stew. It's one of my best dishes."

"Perfect."

Cage came in bringing the barn smell with him. Hannah's nose wrinkled.

"Oh by the way, we drew the name for you, the person you are cooking for is Sheriff Campbell." Bernice's nasally voice rasped on her nerves.

Cage froze and muttered an expletive and stomped back out the door.

What was that about?

Three sets of eyes watched her closely for a reaction.

"Good, I've met the sheriff."

Mrs. McCormack pushed up but failed to rise. "Excuse me, I must go and lie down." Hannah jumped up to help, but she waved her off.

For a brief second Hannah thought the older woman looked upset. Could that be tears? She looked angry.

"Well." Bernice rose. "Carter will be anxious to get back to town. Thank you so much for the coffee."

"Nice meeting you, miss." Carter beamed his gap-toothed smile.

Bernice gave her a bone-crushing hug.

Hannah stood on the back stoop to see them off. As she waved, she wondered why the atmosphere had changed when the sheriff was mentioned. She liked the sheriff.

***

Cage frowned as he watched the visitors leave. He stood in the corral by the barn where he had been inspecting one of the horse's legs. When Hannah came out onto the porch to see her guests off, he admired her form as the wind caught her dress and molded the fabric to her curves. She was small, but she was all woman. Their eyes caught and lingered for a brief moment. He couldn't tear his gaze away. Finally, she turned and went inside. She stirred him. Cage couldn't deny it.

So, she would have supper with the sheriff. He wondered how he could stop it. He disliked Mitch Campbell with a passion. He stomped his booted foot and the horse shied.

Mama would be upset if he ever said it out loud. Christians weren't supposed to hate, but he'd been cheated and neglected. Everything that should have been Cage's had been handed to Mitch and the man didn't appreciate it. So why shouldn't he feel loathing toward him? Mitch had a mean streak that he delighted in showing toward Cage when others weren't around. Mitch strutted around town in his sheriff's badge all puffed up and important, when he had a beautiful ranch that his daddy owned, full of fine horses and cattle. Yet, he wasn't the least bit interested in ranching. The man made Cage's blood boil, and he certainly didn't want to see Hannah tangled up with him. He stamped out of the corral and slammed the gate.

Chapter Nine

Hannah's mind swirled with thoughts of the coming afternoon of cooking, then spending the meal she created with the handsome sheriff. He always made her feel safe. He had a manly essence about him that pleased her.

She knew her mother's stew recipe by heart and Mrs. McCormack helped get the ingredients peeled and ready in a large pot. Again, the older woman's efforts weren't perfect, but Hannah didn't care because the therapy helped Mrs. McCormack's brain gain back what the stroke had taken. The more she used the effected side, the better her mind would recover.

"This meal of stew will taste delicious, dear."

"Thank you, Mrs. McCormack. Are you sure I can't pay you for the ingredients?"

"No, dear, don't be silly. You'll hurt my feelings."

"The bread smells ready." Hannah went to the stove to check on it. She opened the oven with the flowered apron she wore and pulled one loaf to the front.

"No dear, that needs about five more minutes."

Hannah wondered if she would ever be as good a cook as her mother and Mrs. McCormack. She still needed to tap it to hear if it sounded hollow, then she could be sure the bread was ready to come out. Others could tell by just looking at the color.

"I hope you made lots of bread, dear. Micajah loves fresh bread and preserves."

Hannah smiled. The son and mother had a wonderful relationship that she envied. She wondered if she would be with them long enough to be included in their warm bond.

They worked on, taking the bread out when it was ready. Then Hannah thought to ask, "You never speak of Mr. McCormack. Am I being too personal to ask, has he passed?"

A moment went by before the answer came. "It's no secret in these parts. There is no Mr. McCormack. Long ago, I had a beau whom I loved very much. Micajah is the result of a young girl's foolishness. His father went on to marry a woman who is very rich in land, cattle and horses."

The room became quiet then, and Hannah thought she had overstepped her bounds. A sad faraway look had overtaken Mrs. McCormack's face. They finished the stew and the older woman went to lie down until noon.

***

Cage came in for the noonday meal to the rich aroma of fresh-baked bread. His stomach growled and he smiled in anticipation. His mother sat at her usual spot at the table. Cage's mouth watered as Hannah set the meal before him. After Mrs. McCormack said grace, Hannah smiled. "How is the calf today?"

"She's doing well."

"I must come out and see her for a minute or two later."

"You can see her when you come to milk Bessy before supper."

Moments passed, then Hannah spoke up. "I need to make a confession." She lowered her head. "I have no idea how to milk a cow. Couldn't you do it?" she asked, turning her most pleading eyes on him.

"I'll show you how," Cage met her eyes with a determined stare.

She expelled the breath she held. His tone warned there would be no debate. She looked to his mother for support, but she looked away.

Rising from the table, she walked to the stove. He saw disappointment and angst evident on her face. Cage sat in his chair and stoically finished his meal. She would milk the cow.

***

At four o'clock Cage came to the door and Hannah followed him out to the barn for her first milking lesson. Her feet dragged through the dirt like a man walking his last steps to the gallows. Her stomach still held the knots that twisted tighter all afternoon.

As she trudged dutifully behind him, she realized this man had no idea how abhorrent this task would be for her. First, she hated the smells of the barn itself. Second, the big animal frightened her. And third, she had no desire to learn what this man was determined to teach her.

They neared the door of the huge building and the odor of dung and animal sweat wafted out to greet her.

"Please, Mr. McCormack, wait."

Her employer turned impatient black eyes on her.

"I came here to look after your mother, and I really don't feel this should be a part of my duties. Can't you hire someone?"

He huffed out an angry breath. "My mother was a great help, and I need you to take up some of her chores." He swept his hand through his black hair and waited, the delay clearly annoyed him.

When she didn't answer he said, "Miss Wall, I cannot handle the entire farm on my own. I don't have money to hire someone. Right now there is a sick cow that needs my attention, but I am taking the necessary time to teach you this simple task."

Setting her face with a thin-mouthed expression, she gestured toward the barn. "Then lead the way."

She stomped into the dim light behind him. Her small legs taking three steps to his one as he led her to Bessy's stall.

Reality hit as she watched him pull a stool out of the corner and position it near the cow's hindquarter. She swallowed hard.

"Come around here so you can see what I'm doing." His voice was gentle now as he indicated a spot beside him for her to stand.

Tremors of fear rippled through her, but she moved up to his right by the cow's big belly.

"Milking is very simple. You put your hands like this around two of her teats. She is full at this time of day and the milk should come down easy. You move your hands and the milk will squirt into the pail."

His hands pulled downward and milk zinged a bell-like sound when it hit the empty metal pail with force. He continued a few strokes then looked up at her.

She nodded and he stood and let her sit down. As she balanced on the small stool, she was overwhelmed by the size of Bessy who now loomed high above her.

"Now grab hold and begin milking." His rich, baritone voice encouraged from beside her.

It took everything in her to touch the cow's private parts. She was shocked at how warm Bessy was and how hairy her underside felt. She wrinkled her nose, determined now to finish this job and go back inside.

Please Lord get me through this.

She squeezed and pulled down hard as Cage had done. The cow bellowed and stomped her foot, narrowly missing Hannah. She teetered back to avoid being hurt and almost lost her balance. Blindly, she reached out and grabbed a strangle hold on Cage's leg.

She looked up to see a wide grin on his face. "What are you doing?"

"Milking your cow, sir," she ground out. She released his leg and righted herself on the stool.

"Well, not like that." His voice stern.

She was surprised to look up and see him still smiling. He came down on his haunches in the straw beside her and grabbed her hands.

"Here, let me show you. You hold like this. Squeeze, then gently pull down. Don't yank." His soothing voice spoke near her ear warming her cheek and causing her heart to flutter.

He held his hands over hers and illustrated for her the motion she needed. Her heart thrummed at his touch. With his face right beside hers she could feel his warmth too close to her side. His male scent evident in the close quarters kept distracting her. How was she supposed to concentrate when his deep voice was just above a whisper near her ear? And she could feel the heat from his hands radiating up her arms.

He got up suddenly. "You okay now?"

"Yes." She nodded, missing his warmth as he moved away.

She followed his instruction and milk squirted into the pail. Cage gave a terse nod and he walked into the next stall. Small amounts of milk dribbled out as she mimicked the action he had taught her. It had become much too close in her stall. It was a good thing he had left.

***

Cage stepped away and tried to get hold of himself. He grabbed a nearby pitchfork and threw hay around. That woman was going to be trouble. And woman trouble was trouble he didn't need. She was stirring feelings in him that he did <u>not</u> want to deal with.

She's just here to help Mama, he reminded himself. He would not get involved with her no matter how twisted up she made him feel. When she had grabbed his legs, he'd about died. The sensation shooting through him of longing caught him off guard. Then he had seen the humor in what she had done, yanking so hard on poor Bessy and he grinned.

"Yow," came the female voice from the next stall.

"What's wrong?" he called over.

"Her tail. She's swatting me with her tail."

Cage put down the pitchfork and walked over to see if he could help.

"I'll hold it this time, but after this you'll have to deal with it."

He stood behind the cow, grinning to himself, as he held the waving tail, so Hannah could finish milking. When he thought about it, she was a little thing. He studied the determined look on her pretty round face. Her cheeks were flushed with a rosy hue, her lips pursed as she concentrated. She really wasn't very good at milking, but she'd improve with practice.

She stopped for a moment and wiped sweat from her brow with the sleeve of her forearm. He knelt beside her. The fragrance of roses wafted around him. There was that feeling again. He jumped to his feet. Yes, this woman was going to be hard to resist.

Chapter Ten

Hannah heard the back door open and began ladling stew into bowls for the noon meal. Cage shed his coat and hat at the door and was at his place at the table when she placed the savory dish in front of him. Mrs. McCormack said grace in her slurred melodic voice. They needed no conversation as they ate in companionable silence.

"I see you're goin' into town later." With an abrupt motion, Cage indicated Hannah's dress hung over the back of a nearby chair.

She glanced up with a spoonful of stew half way to her lips. "Yes, I'm still one of the brides."

"Can't you just stay here and care for my mother and forget about all that, for now?"

She lowered her spoon into her bowl her lips drew into a thin line. "Not unless I have the money to pay for the train ticket the men advanced for my passage out here." She gave him time to digest that, and then added. "Besides,

I came out here to find a husband not be a nurse. I could have saved a long journey if being a nurse was my intention."

He stopped eating his stew and looked thoughtful for a moment.

"I see." He exchanged a glance with his mother. "You watch yourself with him, then."

Apprehension caught in her chest, and she swallowed hard.

"Do you mean with the sheriff?"

Cage abruptly rose and picked up his plate.

"That's exactly who I mean." With that, he put his dish in the tub and left.

Bewildered, Hannah turned to Mrs. McCormack.

"What was that all about?"

She shuffled to her feet. "Sorry dear, Micajah will have to explain. It's not my place."

She carried her plate to the counter and headed off for her afternoon nap. Annoyed and puzzled, knowing she had struck a nerve, Hannah cleared the table putting food aside for the McCormack's evening meal and prepared for her supper in town.

***

She sat in the closed-in front porch and watched the lane for Mr. Henderson to approach. Her good dress lay wrapped in a sheet to keep the dust off during the trip to town. The pot of stew and bowl of rice pudding sat ready inside the cellar door. She bit her nails and waited.

Soon Bear started to bark, and she gathered her things. When the wagon pulled up to the back door, she was surprised and happy to see Bernice and a chaperone had come with Mr. Henderson.

"Hannah you're not wearing that cotton dress to supper are you?"

"No, I'll cook in this dress, and then I'll put my good dress on. See? I have it wrapped."

When Mr. Henderson had all of her things in the wagon and helped her up onto the high seat, Bernice hugged her hard. As much as Bernice's demeanour and voice annoyed her, Hannah was glad to see a familiar face.

The ride to town went by pleasantly. Hannah enjoyed the endless open prairie. The sky drifted with small clouds that stretched from one horizon to the other. A hawk led the way for a distance then lit on a bush by a pond. The folk on the prairie called the body of water a slough. Ducks diving in the pond sent widening circles that caught and reflected the sunlight on its surface.

They approached Pine Creek; Hannah could see it in the distance long before they reached it, a cluster of trees and whitewashed buildings, the grain elevator standing taller than the rest. The bare wooden-cross of the church, stood tall and proud as well.

The now familiar tension and apprehension filled her midsection. It started with butterflies in her stomach. One thought of Harland waiting for her was all it took. The conversation between Carter and Bernice muffled as fear filled her chest like rain filling a puddle. It made it hard to breathe.

Would he be there waiting?

"Are there any strangers in town?" she blurted, cutting Bernice's sentence in half.

Both Carter and Bernice turned, their companionable conversation brought to a halt.

"No, why do you ask? You look worried." Bernice patted her arm.

"There's no one gotten off the train, Miss Wall." Carter reassured her with certainty.

Relief slammed into her. "Oh, good. I just wondered."

Hannah tried to appear nonchalant. She laced her gloved fingers in her lap wishing her voice hadn't sounded quite so strained. Carter was the agent at the train station in town. He would notice a stranger right away.

Relieved, she tried to take deep breaths and calm herself as they traveled the last distance into Pine Creek.

Children and barking dogs greeted them as the wagon pulled up in front of the hotel. The ruckus the dogs made brought some of the brides onto the porch.

Carter helped both ladies down and Hannah was swarmed by the eager brides.

"How are you?" Mary the pretty, dark-haired woman asked.

"Fine."

"How is Mrs. McCormack?" Lily, the strawberry blonde, asked.

"She's fairing well."

The questions continued as they entered the cool interior of the hotel. Carter and Bernice followed with Hannah's supplies. She sent them a thankful smile as the tide of brides swept her away.

After enjoying tea and catching up with her friends, Hannah began her preparations in the kitchen. Nellie supplied the garlic and raisins she hadn't brought with her. She and her gentleman would have the dining room to themselves. Soon it was time to dress for her date. Bernice allowed Hannah to use her room.

As she fixed her hair, Hannah worried if the dress she had was suitable and if the sheriff would like it.

"Oh, I love your dress, Hannah. I have a ribbon just that color. Let's fashion it around your throat. Chokers are in all the catalogues now, you know?"

As grating as Bernice could be, Hannah began genuinely to like the kind-hearted girl. She thanked her and gave her a big hug before leaving to serve supper. Her nervousness increased as she slipped down the stairs.

Hannah carried the tureen of stew while Nellie preceded her into the dining room. Her breath caught as she saw Sheriff Mitch Campbell. He waited at the beautifully set table.

Bone china and crystal Nellie's family had brought from England set an elegant mood. Scented candles flickered and matched the yellow linen napkins. These sat atop a white, lacy, crochet tablecloth.

He stood when she approached, and her heart sped up when she noticed his clean white shirt and dress pants. His black hair, recently cut and slicked back with hair tonic, attested to the time he had taken with his appearance.

She set the large bowl on the table. She lost herself in the warm chocolate of his eyes.

Nellie made proper introductions. "Sheriff Mitch Campbell may I present Miss Hannah Wall." She wasn't aware that they had already met.

He lifted her hand and kissed it. She thrilled at his finesse. He seated her at the table and after taking his seat, he spoke.

"Please call me Mitch, Miss Wall."

A flush warmed Hannah's face. "And you must call me Hannah."

She reached for his plate and filled it with the stew and the bread she had baked. The aroma was delicious.

Mitch reached out both hands to her. "May I say grace?"

She placed her hands in his palms. "Yes, please."

"Father in heaven, please be with us now as we enjoy this meal together. Bless this food to our bodies and bless those who prepared it. Amen."

Hannah marvelled at the words in Mitch's prayer. It was so much more polished than the one Cage had mumbled the other day.

"This tastes wonderful, Miss Wall." He met her eyes and smiled. "Hannah."

She bit her lip. "Thank you. It was my mother's recipe."

"How are you liking, Pine Creek?"

"I found the prairie vast and unnerving at first. However, I quite like it now. The people here in town have been very welcoming. Nellie and Mrs. McCormack are especially dear."

Mitch choked and her eyes flew to his face. "Are you all right?"

"Yes, yes, I'm fine." He waved he was fine and picked up his water glass.

Time passed, as they ate on in companionable conversation. Hannah enjoyed the ease she felt with this man, much different from the constant tension she felt in Cage's presence.

"I need the sheriff, right now." An excited male voice yelled from the hallway.

Mitch jumped to his feet.

"I best see what this is about. I'll be right back."

Hannah ate the last forkful of her meal as the drama at the door unfolded.

Nellie tried to keep the man from disturbing Mitch's meal. The man was not about to be put off. As Nellie tried to block him, he thwarted her by speaking louder.

Moments later Mitch came back.

"There is a problem at the livery. A dispute over a horse. Guns are drawn. I better go."

He glanced down at his almost empty plate. "Maybe we can enjoy dessert when I get back."

"Certainly." She whispered, afraid her disappointment had been evident in her voice.

His eyes met hers in apology. He gathered his hat and coat from a nearby chair. The star on his coat shone in the candlelight as he put on his jacket then rushed out the door.

Hannah rose and cleared the table. Nellie came and helped.

"I'm sorry, Hannah. Let's you and I have a cup of tea while you wait for the sheriff."

They left the dishes soaking and came back with their cups. They passed several minutes exchanging pleasantries then Hannah broached the subject that had been bothering her.

"Nellie, when I mention the sheriff out at the McCormack ranch, they reacted strangely. Is there a history there that I need to know about?"

"Yes, I'm sorry, Hannah. I should have mentioned this before. Cage and Mitch are half-brothers."

Hannah sat stunned as Nellie sipped her tea.

"It's believed that Mitch's father is also Cage's father."

It made sense. They both had the same black hair and dark-chocolate brown eyes. But there the similarities stopped. Mitch was as tall as Cage but large with a barrel chest. Cage was whip-thin but muscular.

"Cage dislikes Mitch." Nellie went on. "Cage was born into comparative poverty while his father left his mother alone and pregnant to go on to marry Louise, Mitch's mother. By marrying her, Byron became rich in land, cattle and horses. Cage hates that Mitch has wonderful farmland and animals, and instead of embracing it like Cage would, Mitch chose to turn his back on it and be sheriff."

Nellie stopped suddenly and raised her hands to her mouth. "I fear, I've said too much."

"It's all right Nellie, I needed to know."

Another five minutes passed while they changed the subject and discussed the burgeoning romance between Bernice and Carter. As Nellie spoke, Hannah processed the information she had just been given. Perhaps this is where Cage's bitterness stemmed from? Resentment toward his father leaving his mother on a poor piece of land in poverty and then going on to marry a rich woman for her holdings. And that bitterness had transferred to the son who had everything but didn't care. She could see how Cage and his mother left to fend for themselves and getting comparatively nowhere would cause resentment and strong emotions.

★★★

Mitch returned and Nellie served the rice pudding Hannah made. He watched her across the table as she delicately spooned it into her mouth. She had made the dessert just the way he liked it, with lots of raisins and sprinkled with cinnamon on top.

She created a longing in him. Of all the brides, she was the one he wanted, and it galled him that Cage had her all to himself on his forsaken excuse for a ranch.

She smiled across the table at him.

Yes, she would be his bride. He would make sure of it.

"Hannah, this is the best rice pudding I have ever tasted."

"Thank you."

See the way her eyes fluttered. Yes, flattery worked with her. He smiled satisfied he could win her.

Carter entered the dining room. "Evening, folks." He doffed his hat. "The buggy's waitin' when Miss Hannah's ready. If we leave soon, I can be home before dark."

With that, Mitch rose and pulled Hannah's chair out for her.

"Thanks, Carter, we'll be along shortly."

Left alone in the dining room, Mitch drank in the sight of this delicate woman. He helped her with her shawl, then turned her to face him and pulled her to him.

His mouth pressed down on hers, her eyes widened in disbelief. Even though she stiffened, he closed his eyes and laid claim to her lips. He devoured them not wanting to stop, trying without success to part her lips, then pulled away. Had she been pushing at him? Pushing him away? Here was a woman not used to the passionate kisses he was wont to giving.

Hannah stepped away and blushed a pretty pink. Her eyes opened wide with wonder. *Ah, yes, she would be his prize.*

He offered his arm and walked her out to the waiting carriage.

"Carter will escort you home. I can't leave town for too long at night."

"Yes, of course." She twisted her gloves in her hands. "Thank you for a wonderful meal."

"You're welcome."

He helped her into the buggy where Bernice waited to accompany her home.

Both women waved as Carter slapped the reins, and they were off. Mitch stood silent as the buggy carried her back to Cage. He hated the thought and wanted to know if Cage cared for her. If Cage did, he would have to work fast to take her first.

***

"Doc lent us his buggy." Bernice hooked Hannah's arm.

"Nice."

"How was your meal?"

"Good, we were interrupted once, but it went very well."

Bernice chattered as the prairie miles passed by. Hannah thought about the kiss. It didn't seem proper for Mitch to accost her that way. They hardly knew each other. She was a little embarrassed by it. It had been much too passionate for the first time as well.

They would soon be home to the ranch. Hannah wondered how Cage would treat her. Would he feel she had been consorting with the enemy?

Chapter Eleven

Pain roiled in Cage's stomach as he thought of his half-brother Mitch with Hannah.

It wasn't jealousy. No. He just thought Hannah deserved better.

He whistled to the black and white dog. "Get on back up here, Bear. We've got work to do."

After checking on his mother, he saddled one of his three painted horses, Calliope. Cage and the dog went to check on his cattle. He had to keep busy or this day would never end.

The afternoon dragged on as he waited for Hannah to return. His insides stayed in knots the entire day.

Why did he even care what she did or who she was with today? What was she to him? His mother's nurse.

No, she was more than that. She was special. Something about her drew him like moths to the lantern light. He wished to protect her, as a male bird guards his mate on the nest. And yes, he wanted her to be the one on his nest.

Where had that thought come from? He turned his horse and went to the barn.

As he unsaddled his horse, he shook his head, and admitted he cared for Hannah. It would mean a lot to him to keep her here. He needed to let the mayor know that he wanted to throw his name into the ring with the rest of the grooms.

He spent the rest of the day looking after his mother and waiting for Carter to bring Hannah back. He paced incessantly.

Finally, a couple of hours before dark, Bear began barking and Cage went to the window. A cloud of dust surrounded Doc's shiny buggy as it rocked up the lane.

"She's back," he called to his mother as he put his jacket on.

A happiness he had not felt for years flooded him, and he smiled.

***

Hannah wrung her hands and waited for the carriage to stop by the back door.

She widened her eyes in surprise when she saw Cage waiting on the porch with his arms across his chest. The moment the buggy stopped, he stepped forward with a warm smile.

Her small hands disappeared in the fabric of his jacket as he helped her down and for the briefest of moments she saw something appealing in his eyes. His muscular hands lingered on her waist longer than necessary. The embrace made her heart skip a beat.

"Welcome home."

"Thank you." Her fingers uncurled from the fabric of his coat just before he released her.

"How was the drive, Carter?"

Hannah looked up into Cage's dark chocolate eyes as he spoke to Carter.

"Fine."

"Will you stay for coffee?" Cage invited.

"No thanks, I gotta be back b'fore dark." He released the brake.

"Well, thank you for bringin' Hannah back safe."

"No problem. Bye, now." Carter flicked the reins.

"Thank you." Hannah and Cage both called together as the buggy made a circle and left the yard.

The warmth of the house met her as she entered with Cage on her heels. She thought she heard him humming.

This wasn't the dark, somber man she had left hours before.

She liked this change.

Hannah removed her coat, too warm now, and by the time she reached the kitchen table where Mrs. McCormack waited, Cage had a steaming cup of coffee poured for her.

"How was your meal, dear?" The elder woman's eyes held interest as Hannah looked into their depths.

"It was lovely."

"Did Nellie have the things you needed?"

"Yes. She was very gracious and helped a lot. She let me use her best china and we lit scented candles."

"That sounds nice."

"It was." Hannah turned to Cage who was leaning against the counter watching her. "Have you both had your supper?"

"Yes, it was good. Thank you. Mama is probably tired but wouldn't go to bed until you came home."

"Yes, I'll go as soon as we finish our coffee." The frail woman murmured in her slightly slurred speech.

A loving smile passed between mother and son.

Hannah helped the elderly woman prepare for bed. She gasped when the kitchen was immaculate when she returned. The cups sat drying on the cupboard and the sugar bowl put away.

Delighted, Hannah saw that Cage had "locked the doors" and he had banked the stove with wood for the night.

When she climbed into her bed later, she was weary but happy. She said prayers, then pondered the time she had spent with Mitch. The meal had gone well, and she had enjoyed his company.

But what kind of man would kiss a lady so passionately when they had only recently met? She wished she had someone with which she could talk these things over. Was his behaviour something she should worry about?

And what had gotten into Cage while she was gone those few hours? Suddenly, he was attentive and helpful. It was nice.

There was talk of a ladies' choice picnic on Saturday. Each bride would ask the potential groom of her choice to escort her on a picnic to the school grounds. They would all be there at the same time and eat their meal somewhere in the yard alone with their gentleman, then all gather afterward for dessert. Nellie had agreed to deliver it.

Her mind drifted off, wondering who to choose for the occasion. It should be someone she wanted to get to know better. She was already getting to know the sheriff. Someone else, but who?

***

At breakfast the next morning, Cage broached the subject that was on his mind. He knew the city girl wouldn't like this, but it had to be done, and soon.

"Hannah, the garden needs to be planted. I'll work up the soil this morning. Then this afternoon you can plant it."

Her eyes flew to his face. "I've never planted a garden before."

Cage blew out a long breath. "I can show you while Mama naps this afternoon."

She nodded. She didn't look too happy.

***

Cage impatiently scuffed his feet in the garden plot at the side of the house anticipating Hannah's arrival. He shifted from foot to foot waiting. The toes of his boots picked up more dirt the longer he stood. The spring day was warm heating his back, and he rolled up his shirtsleeves.

He heard the door bang, and seconds later, Hannah appeared from the back of the building. Cage tried hard to suppress a grin as he took a good look at what she wore. She had an old floppy hat of his mother's, long sleeves with a shawl over her shoulders and gloves.

It won't be long before she sheds that get-up. He grinned mischievously at the thought.

She had almost reached him where he stood in the freshly tilled earth when their eyes met and she gave him a forced smile. At least she was willing to try.

A toad hopped out of the grass she was passing through. She shrieked and took three hurried steps to him.

Without thinking, his arm encircled her and pulled her to his side.

One arm came around his waist, and she hung on.

"It's just a toad. You're all right."

"Oh, I'm sorry. I didn't know what it was," she backed away her embarrassment painted all over her alluring face.

As she stepped away, he missed her warmth. The air around him lingered with her scent.

"Come." He led her to one edge of the plot. "I'll show you what you need to do."

"These are the seeds, and we'll plant them in straight rows. You press your finger into the dirt. Then put a seed into the hole and cover it. I can't believe you've never done this. Did your parents not have a garden back in Boston?"

"No, we lived in the heart of town. I helped my grandfather plant potatoes once. He dug the hole, and I placed the potato in."

"Well good. That's a start. Listen, you are going to have to take those gloves off and that shawl is going to dangle down and get in your way."

She huffed but did take off her shawl and gloves then rolled up her sleeves. She kept wiping her hands off on her apron after each seed she planted.

"Hannah, there is no way around it. Your hands are going to get dirty."

He watched her peer down at her hand as she rubbed it on her apron. She smiled up at him. He could tell she saw the humour in what she was doing.

His eyes locked with hers and he felt a camaraderie that hadn't been there before.

They worked together and after a time it looked to Cage as if she enjoyed herself. They had half the garden planted when Cage suggested. "Let's take a break. My back needs a rest."

"Mine, too."

He led her to the old well. Cage pumped water, filled a dipper and held it out for her.

"You've lived here your whole life, haven't you?" Hannah scooted her bottom onto the well's wooden platform as she wiped water from her chin.

Cage joined her on the well. "Yes. I have no desire to be anywhere else. I love this place, the cattle and the horses."

"It's a big change for me."

"I can see that." He smiled down at her.

She looked down at her work-roughened hands.

"You don't mind the hard work and constant wind."

"No, it's the pull of the land. It becomes a part of you."

"I like the prairie. It holds its own beauty."

"I'm glad that you can see that. A lot of Easterners get here and can't wait to go back." He hoped she would never want to leave.

"I like living here."

"You don't miss the trees?"

"Well, perhaps, but I love the sky here, it's alive. The landscape is constantly changing with different shaped clouds everyday. We don't notice it back east the way you do here. The forests hide the sky there."

"Well, maybe we'll make a prairie girl of you, yet."

He rose, slapping his gloves on his knee and walked back to finish planting.

***

Hannah watched Cage walk to the garden plot.

Maybe he was right. Maybe this is what God wanted for her life, to be a prairie bride.

Now she needed to decide on a husband and wait for him to ask her to marry him. And pray that Harland would never find her.

Chapter Twelve

Hannah's weekdays had fallen into a routine. Up at the first sound of Fredrick, the rooster's, crowing. Help Mrs. McCormack, who now insisted on being called Charlotte, get dressed and to the privy first thing. Cook breakfast and have it ready when Cage came in from his morning chores.

"Morning, ladies."

Hannah stood at the stove flipping flapjacks when Cage took his place at the table. Charlotte sat across from him humming softly to herself, sipping coffee.

"Good morning, how is our calf faring today?" Hannah placed Cage's plate, stacked with golden pancakes, before him.

"He's doing fine for arriving early. We should have a lot more coming soon."

"Micajah, Hannah needs to do laundry today. Would you be a dear and get the water on the stove after breakfast?"

"Yes, she can finish planting the garden while it's heating."

As Hannah came back to the table with her plate, she looked for the warmth in Cage's eyes that had been so noticeable yesterday. It wasn't there. He was all business this morning. Her shoulders sagged and her head dropped.

***

The women left the water to get hot on the stove and donned their jackets and floppy hats. Charlotte laughed at Hannah in her borrowed old woman's sunhat.

"Don't let her overdo it," Cage whispered to Hannah.

"I won't."

Hannah watched Charlotte closely and was happy to see an improvement in her mobility. She was using her cane less and the strength was returning. Her leg had improved. Now, if only her arm would recover. They walked arm in arm out to the garden.

The sun was warm on Hannah's back as she dug the holes and Charlotte placed the potatoes inside. It was difficult sometimes for Charlotte to place the potato properly but Hannah knew that as the stroke victim struggled, she was also retraining her brain and regenerating what she had lost.

"Hannah, I keep thinking about what we talked about the other day."

"Oh, what was that? Mrs. McCor. . . I mean Charlotte."

"About Micajah and his father."

"Yes, I remember." She stepped closer interested to hear more.

"I wish there was a way for them to have a relationship. Cage has built up such resentment toward him and his family. I haven't been able to make any headway."

Hannah realized she was talking about Mitch and his parents, Louise and Byron Campbell.

"Sometimes these things can only be handled by God, in His time and with prayer." Hannah said leaning on the shovel.

"Yes, I suppose you're right. It's just that Micajah holds such bitterness inside."

"Well, we can certainly pray about that."

"Yes, we can." She met Hannah's eyes and briefly gave her hand a squeeze.

Cage came by and insisted his mother rest. Continuing her gardening, Hannah prayed she would find a way to reconcile Cage and his father.

It seemed an impossible task.

***

After Charlotte had gone in for a rest, Hannah worked on in the garden. She straightened for a moment and marvelled that her garden now contained straight, orderly rows of peas, carrots, cucumbers, potatoes, corn, onions and beans buried under the earth.

She gave her back a rest and surveyed her handiwork when Bear nudged her for a pat. She was delighted when he let her pet him. The softness of his fur made her want to bury her face in it.

Oh, why not?

She bent her knees and allowed herself to cuddle in the dog's soft neck.

"You'll let me know if Harland comes, won't you, boy? Maybe you'll even bite him if he tries to hurt me."

A cough sounded behind her and her head shot up. Cage stood in the corral, with the horses, watching. Their eyes met and he smiled then turned away and disappeared into the barn.

Hannah sensed when Harland found her she wouldn't have to face him alone. A new confidence filled her heart and her muscles relaxed for the first time since arriving.

As she finished the last rows of beans, she pondered who to invite to the picnic. The pastor was handsome, but he wasn't one of the grooms. Carter was a nice man, but it would be disloyal to send word to him when Bernice was so interested in him. There was Scott, the bartender, but he was young, and she didn't want to show interest when she had no intension of him becoming her groom. Then there was the suitor from the reception, but there was something desperate and clingy about him.

As she bent to put the final few seeds in the soil, a shadow fell across the ground. She looked up into Cage's face, and she spoke before she thought. "I need someone to take me to the picnic on Saturday at the school grounds."

"All right, I want to go to town anyway," Cage said in his usual gruff manner and started to walk away.

He didn't understand. He thought she just wanted a ride. "We're supposed to share a meal together," she called out in a rush.

He looked back over his shoulder. "Yes."

He turned and kept walking. Her heart did a happy dance. Oh my.

Hannah watched his retreating back wanting to laugh and cry. She was so surprised he had agreed so easily. Her feet scuffed the dirt in a jig and then it hit her.

Her heart dropped as she wondered if spending a whole afternoon with him would be a good idea. He could heat up and get mad so easily.

Oh Heavenly Father, what have I done?

***

Hannah checked on the laundry water. It was hot enough to get the job done.

"Soap's in the pantry and the wash tub is hanging on a nail by the back door." Charlotte said coming out of the parlour.

"Thanks, I'll get the tub." Hannah turned to go outside.

"I'll get the soap and the scrub board." Charlotte went to the pantry.

Hannah lifted the pans of hot water with a rolled up towel to protect her hands from the heated handles. Her eyes widened at how heavy it was and she stumbled and sloshed water on the floor.

She left Charlotte to sit and scrub the clothes clean. It was hard work and the soap was abrasive on the hands, but was a task Charlotte could handle.

Hannah grabbed a bone from the sideboard and carried the empty pots outside to refill them for rinse water. As she walked across the yard in her shawl, she enjoyed the spring sunshine. Bear came out of nowhere to join her.

"Here, boy, I saved this for you."

He sat up on his haunches barking expectantly until she let him have the bone she had brought out for him.

He wasn't the frightening beast she had first thought. Her original fear had dissipated. It warmed her heart to have made friends. She gave him a quick pat on the head and smiled as he trotted into the shade of one of the poplar trees to enjoy his treat.

She lowered the bucket down the well and her arms strained at the effort it took to haul the heavy pail back out of the deep cavern.

Suddenly, she wasn't alone. The manly scent of Cage teased her senses as his shadow fell across the place where she stood.

"Here, Hannah, let me do that."

Cage grabbed the rope above her hands and pulled the pail up. Sweat had broken out on her forehead, and she stepped back to watch him as she wiped it off with a hanky that she carried in her skirt pocket.

Muscles bunched under the cotton material of Cage's blue shirt. His upper arms strained, while he pulled hard on the rope to bring the bucket up to the surface. She noticed his callused hands as he filled the pots for her.

For a brief moment, she remembered those hands on her waist as he helped her down from the wagon. How he had steadied her and her hands had grabbed the soft material of his worn shirt. It gave her a pleasant memory she wouldn't mind repeating.

"Come on, I'll help you carry these." He turned and she flushed at the thoughts she had been having.

She followed him, happily hauling the smaller pan.

"I'm goin' to town. Is there anything either of you need?" he asked, setting the pots on the stove to heat for rinse water.

Hannah made a list and handed it to him. Fear gripped her. Her first thought was to demand she go with him. This would be the first time she and Charlotte would be alone on the farm.

"Will you be long?"

"No, just in and right back again."

She chewed her lip in concern for a moment then realized she could handle it with God's help.

Cage left and she busied herself with rinsing the clothes and taking them out to hang on the line.

As she pinned the clothes to the cord strung between the back porch and a tree, Cage left on his horse. She called Bear over and felt better when he settled himself near her feet.

She was hanging out the second basket when a stranger approached on horseback in a cloud of dust coming from the opposite direction of Pine Creek. Apprehension filled her. Then she realized that Harland or his men would come here from town not from the route that this man had taken.

Hannah guessed the man who rode up, was probably in his mid sixties, a distinguished man with graying black hair. Thinly built like Cage but thicker in the middle. Perhaps a businessman or wealthy farmer.

"Hello, miss."

"Good day, sir. Are you here to see the McCormacks?" She held tight to Bear's thick mane as he growled low at the intruder. This man obviously didn't call often.

"No, miss, I was out riding and thought I'd stop by. You're new in these parts."

"Yes, sir."

"You married to Micajah then?"

"Oh no, sir." She felt the heat rise in her cheeks. "I'm here to care for Mrs. McCormack."

"I heard she suffered a stroke. How is she now?"

Hannah instantly liked this big friendly man. His warm dark eyes and deep voice made her comfortable. Bear had settled and was wagging his tail.

"She's faring well. Would you like to come in for a visit? I could make a pot of coffee."

"Oh no, I can't," he said, suddenly looking ill at ease. "Well, miss. It's been nice talking to you."

"It was nice that you rode in. May I tell Mrs. McCormack who stopped by?"

"Just tell her Byron asked about her." With that, he kicked his horse and left the way he came at a lope.

Light dawned in Hannah's mind, and she dropped the pants she held as her hand flew to her mouth.

She had just spoken to Cage's father!

She was stunned. She pressed her fingers harder against her mouth. Why had he ridden in and not gone in to visit? Had he seen her and thought he could inquire without having to see Cage or Charlotte? She shook her head wondering.

She stopped to pick up Cage's now dirty trousers out of the prairie dust. Should she mention the visit? He hadn't said not to.

She walked back to the house carrying the soiled pants and the empty hamper. She liked the gentleman she had just met. It would be nice if Cage could see the man's good side.

***

Cage walked into the mercantile with one mission in mind. To buy a new shirt and pants to wear to the picnic. If he was going to escort Hannah, he didn't want her feeling he was the poorest dressed man there. He picked out a soft chambray shirt in a deep green. Then he chose a new pair of denim pants.

He paid for them and put the paper wrapped package in his saddlebags. *If he would spark a girl, he'd do it in fashion.*

He shook his head. That woman had him in knots and thinking crazy thoughts too.

As he rode home, his stomach churned with excitement and he spurred his horse to a gallop. Saturday, he must be on his best behavior.

Chapter Thirteen

Hannah stretched her arms in an effort to awaken. Saturday had finally come. Her room, under the eaves of the house was chilly. Goose bumps on her arms caused her to burrow under the covers as she rolled over. She savored the luxury of laying under the warm covers a moment or two longer.

Excitement coursed through her as she thought of the coming day. At the picnic, she would see all of her friends. She could find out about their quest to find a groom. Had any of them found love?

This mail-order-bride arrangement was risky. The way this group of men handled it was better than when the woman had no choice. Here, there was a chance for women to meet and choose a mate. Many women from the east married a complete stranger who had sent for them, no choice for the woman at all. She doubted she could agree to that. Deep down she was a romantic at heart and wanted to marry someone she loved.

She thought of the sheriff, Mitch Campbell. He was attractive, a big man with a warm smile. Lots of him to love. Although the way he had so savagely kissed her, might appeal to some, her genteel upbringing told her something wasn't quite as it should be. However, she still hoped she would get to see him and talk to him. She was attracted to him and wanted to get to know him better. Odd she thought how a powerful man still had an appeal to her. She found it strange how she could still be drawn to something her spirit cried out no to. After all she was no longer a young and silly girl.

Why was she lying here thinking of him? It should be Cage occupying her mind. He was the one she would spend the day with at the picnic. He was a mystery, gruff and angry at times. But she saw he could love and be gentle too. She thought of how he was with his mother and his animals.

He had even tried to be domestic. She smiled as she remembered the effort he had gone through to make his room welcoming for her. The ill-made bed she had climbed into that first night had cost him time and effort.

She suppressed a grin, stretched and began her morning routine. Yes, it really should be Cage on her mind today.

***

Cage awoke to the sound of the rooster crowing. Anticipation filled him as he dressed and went out the front door to get his chores done. He knew Hannah would still have the doors "locked" with the kitchen chairs in place. If she needed that to feel safe, then he was all right with it. He just made sure his coat and boots were with him on the porch.

He hummed a happy tune as he worked, milking Bessy and feeding the cattle and horses. He knew when he finished that Hannah would have the door "unlocked" and breakfast ready. It mystified him why Hannah had to lock the door. Was she afraid of him?

He hoped the morning went fast. He couldn't wait to spend some special time with her. He wanted to show her he would be a better husband than Mitch could ever be.

He hated that Mitch had taken up with Hannah. They had a meal together, and she had seemed happy when she came home. If Mitch pursued Hannah, there was nothing he could do to stop him. Mitch had more money, more time, more everything and he would have her. What bride wouldn't choose the rich sheriff over a poor dirt farmer?

***

It was time to go. His chest was tight and constricted as he put the horses into their traces and fastened them in. Blood pounded in his ears. Excitement bubbled from within him, making him jittery.

He drove the wagon to the back door where Hannah waited. His mama gave her one last hug at the door. Doc had dropped off his wife to stay with Cage's mother while Doc was off on his rounds. He gave Doc's wife a wave.

Cage jumped down from the buckboard to escort Hannah. His eyes beheld a vision in a flowered dress in shades of brown and orange with ruffles and lace. She had dressed up for him. His lips relaxed into a happy smile.

He took the picnic basket from her and offered his arm. She smiled and slipped her fingers into the crook of his elbow. Her touch burned through his jacket sleeve. Their eyes met and he thought his heart would stop. His hands tightened on her and he took a deep breath as he helped her onto the high wagon seat.

Today, she smelled of vanilla and roses. He had no idea how he could name what the scents were, but as he slapped the reins and gave one last wave to his mother and Doc's wife that is what filled his senses, something pleasant and alluring.

"Are you comfortable?" He glanced away, then watched Bear circle in front of the wagon, barking and wagging his tail.

"Yes. Thank you. It seems Bear wants to come, too." She chuckled.

"Bear, stay." His voice a little more harsh than he intended. Minding his manners and making a good impression would be harder than he thought.

"Look, Miss Wall, rabbits." He pointed to a pair hopping away into the grass.

Her scowl let him know it annoyed her that he had reverted to calling her by her last name. "Oh please, call me Hannah."

"Then, will you call me Cage?"

"Yes. Of course."

Good, that was one thing off the list of what he wanted to accomplish today. If he was going to court her, they needed to drop the formalities.

As they drove along talking, he longed to find a large bump to drive over so he could slip his arm around her. She smelled so good he wanted her closer.

"Your mother loves her life on the farm."

"Yes, she inherited the land when her parents passed. She's lived on that farm all of her life. It's difficult living so far from town, but she never complains."

"You live in contentment there."

As she talked about life on the farm, he noticed her voice sounded angelic and clear. He loved having her all to himself. As she chatted with him, satisfaction and peace filled him and he fought off the moisture that wanted to collect in his eyes. *If only she could always be his.*

They came to Pine Creek, a cluster of buildings nestled in the midst of the vast prairie. With no need to stop in town, Cage drove straight to the school. Nervous anticipation twisted his stomach. Cage worried about Mitch. What if he was at the picnic? Cage knew from past experience Mitch would delight in taking Hannah from him. He had a vision of him sitting all alone on the picnic blanket while Mitch spirited Hannah away. His hands tightened on the reins and his jaw clenched.

The choice between them would be Hannah's.

Please Lord, I need your help. Show me how to make her mine.

***

Hannah's heart sped up as the small school came into view. The building sat alone on the prairie by a small brook. She could tell where the children had been playing. The grass was tramped down, still brown from the winter. Some brides had arrived, chosen spots away from one another, and spread their picnic blankets out.

Anticipation tightened Hannah's chest as Cage drove the wagon up beside the others and parked in the shade provided by the school building. She waved to friends, knowing she'd have time to visit later when they all had dessert together.

She wrung her hands, a nervous habit since childhood, and now her thin cotton gloves were damp with perspiration. She pulled them off as Cage came around the front of the wagon.

He wore crisp new clothes today, a forest green shirt that suited his coloring. His long black hair almost touched his collar, he was clean-shaven, and he smelled faintly of bay rum after-shave.

She stood and returned his smile as his strong hands grasped her waist, and he swung her down.

Hannah's hands clenched the cotton of his shirt, and she savoured the scent of his cologne as he released her. Her heart thrummed a happy rhythm as she took his arm. He carried their picnic basket and blanket and led her to a grassy area under a tree that grew on the bank of the little stream. Hannah spread the blanket in the shade of the poplar tree and patted a spot beside her.

Cage's dark chocolate eyes held hers as he approached. Their shoulders brushed briefly and a thrill ran through her as he sat down next to her. "Thank you Mr.--um. . . Cage. This is a wonderful spot you've chosen."

"We're lucky we arrived early enough to get it before someone else took it."

"I love the rushing of the stream. There is nothing nicer than the sound of water running over rocks."

"It's soothing, isn't it?" Cage settled in and leaned closer, sending warm heat to Hannah's cheeks.

As they watched a brown bird with long legs and beak poke the sandy bank for food, Hannah thought how nice this Cage was. The thunderous dark eyes were gone. And today she heard no sharp edge to his voice.

The lines of his face had relaxed and smoothed. Their conversation was stilted, but that could be nerves.

After several minutes had passed, she asked, "Are you getting hungry?"

"Yes, let's eat."

Hannah unpacked the lunch and they enjoyed coleslaw, potato salad and slices of beef.

"How are you settling in to life on the farm?" Cage took a devilled egg that Hannah had made.

She responded to the warmth in his dark eyes. "I've had a lot to learn in a short time. I'm discovering what I was afraid of at first is really not so daunting."

***

As they discussed how Hannah had made friends with the dog, and lost some of her fear of Bessy and the bugs in the garden, Cage marvelled at how well things were going. Nothing had happened to ruin their time together. He wanted to open his closed heart to her, but found it difficult.

Tender thoughts were a foreign concept to him except where his mother was concerned. He struggled to let go of his inherent anger and let the tenderness come to the surface.

He wanted to be a good suitor, to act the way a gentleman would toward a lady. Opening doors, being attentive, but he could see it was going to take a great effort with so much fury just under the surface. He knew the antagonism he held since childhood wasn't about to disappear overnight.

As his gaze lingered on her petite features and auburn hair that glinted with red highlights caught in the sun, he knew something inside him had changed.

Maybe God could help him rid his heart of the bitterness it carried. Tonight, he would dust off his old Bible and see if he could find what he needed to change, in there.

***

Hannah was giggling now, talking about the night of the skunk attack. "Your mother and I were disgusted to have to use the privy. What a terrible stench."

Laughter shook his shoulders. "Imagine how Bear felt. He took the brunt of it."

"Yes, we don't have a single jar of tomato left after you bathed him to get rid of the odor."

"I should have had you bathe him." His raucous laugh was drawing attention, and they ducked their heads.

"Oh Cage, you wouldn't have." She giggled all the harder, enjoying his teasing.

This new side of Cage was delightful and engaging. He relaxed and leaned back on one elbow. She came closer to hear his every word.

"I've been wondering if you would like to learn to ride one of the horses at the ranch?"

"I hadn't thought of that."

"Dolly, the one with the speckles on her back is gentle," he coaxed with a smile.

"When I was young, I always wanted to learn to ride. But there was never an opportunity living in Boston. Our horse was only trained to pull our buggy." She took one last bite of potato salad. "Some of the girls at school knew how to ride and I always envied them. So, yes, I'd love to learn."

She saw the pleasure infuse Cage's face as he brightened in a smile.

Hannah placed leftovers in the picnic basket as they chatted. The conversation halted when the school bell rang. She looked up to see the mayor waving for them to come to the school. Hannah saw Nellie leaving the yard in her supply wagon. Strange, the pastor rode hunched over on the tailgate. He was leaving early. Lily appeared forlorn, waving goodbye. Something must have happened to ruin their time together.

Cage stood and offered a hand up. She placed her hand in his much larger work-roughened one, and he helped her to her feet. She smoothed her skirt as Cage picked up the blanket. They folded it together, each taking an end, like two women do when taking sheets off the line on washday. As the folds got smaller, they stood closer and closer together until their eyes met. Cage's eyes held the color of warm, rich milk chocolate, so much lighter and softer than before.

"Thank you, Hannah, for a wonderful meal."

His eyes asked permission as he leaned in and placed his mouth fully on hers in the most wonderful kiss Hannah had ever experienced. His lips didn't linger long enough. But as he drew away, she felt the impact right to her toes.

Startled and delighted, she took the arm he offered after he picked up the basket. Hannah's heart soared as they walked from the brook to the school.

A trestle table was set up beside the school in the shade of a tree. Hannah saw places set for all of the brides and their escorts. Mitch stood watching her approach. She felt Cage stiffen beside her.

Chapter Fourteen

The dessert beckoned to them from the long table used to feed the hired men during the harvest. As Cage led Hannah toward it, he was glad that their day together was going so well.

He looked down upon her with fondness and marvelled at the new protective feeling she invoked in him. Never had he allowed anyone except his mother so close. Hannah was like radiant sunshine melting the block of ice that was his heart.

He took her to the wagon first, walking right past Mitch. While he placed the belongings in the back, Hannah spoke to the horse and timidly stroked his nose.

Cage joined her.

"I thought I better get over my fear," she whispered, as if telling a secret. He smiled and more of the ice melted.

She offered Cage her hand and laced fingers with his as they walked to the table.

When he noticed that the only place left at the table was directly across from Mitch, Cage stopped short. He huffed out an angry breath as Hannah pulled on his hand and urged him forward.

He seated Hannah at the bench with an arm at her back to steady her as she settled herself. He stepped over the bench and glared at his half-brother. The bride Mitch was with was not particularly Mitch's usual type and Cage surmised he had accepted her invitation, so he could see Hannah. Cage could see he was going to hone in on his time alone with Hannah. Anger gripped his chest in a painful vise. A nudge from Hannah encouraged him to eat his dessert.

Apple pie, one of his favorites, tasted like sawdust when he took the first bite.

"This is wonderful," Hannah enthused.

Mitch's companion smiled. "Yes, Nellie is a wonderful baker."

"Apple's my favourite," Mitch said, slopping a morsel on his clean white shirt, as his eyes devoured Hannah instead. He noticed Cage watching him and he gave him a big wink.

Cage dropped his fork and it clattered onto his plate. His hands gripped the edge of the table in an effort to anchor himself. He wanted so bad to slap the lustful look off

Mitch's face. A tug at his sleeve broke through his anger. He glanced over and saw the concern in Hannah's beautiful eyes. He breathed deeply. For her, he would not make a scene.

He set his jaw, picked up his fork, and tried to ignore the big lug across from him. Things never changed. This was just like when they were young and attended the same school. Mitch was always baiting him and rubbing his nose in the poverty in which Cage had grown up. Like the time Cage, so proud of the wonderful wooden horse his mother had been able to get for him, found when he took it to school the next day Mitch had a whole herd of new horses.

Cage fought to tamp down all of the old resentment and hurts, but found it difficult.

Mitch had always taken joy in taunting him about the exploits and adventures he and his father had shared and made sure Cage and the others kids knew Cage was a nobody with no father to take him hunting and fishing.

As a boy, he had always been mean and ruthless. Cage had a hard time believing that the man sitting smug faced before him could be any different.

It really burned him that Mitch seemed so interested in Hannah. The man had hardly taken his eyes off her. He was wearing a piece of pie on his crisp white dress shirt to prove it.

Mitch spoke directly to Hannah. "Did you hear the pastor's picnic got cut short?"

"Oh." Hannah looked up wide-eyed.

"Yeah, he got into a nest of bees and got stung."

"That's why I saw him all hunched over on the back of Nellie's wagon." That's what Hannah had witnessed earlier.

"Yep, she took him back to town to doctor him up."

"He must have had a lot of stings." Hannah looked down the length of the table to where Lily sat alone. Hannah's heart went out to the hopeful bride-to-be whose romantic afternoon had ended abruptly.

Cage leaned forward. "Does she have a ride back to town?"

"I don't know," Mitch snapped.

Cage turned to Hannah. "We'll make sure she gets back."

His kind gesture impressed her, and she gave him a warm smile. Funny she had never noticed before just how handsome Cage truly was.

He sat so rigid beside her, his jaw set, his hostile eyes fixed on Mitch. She could see he wanted to fight with Mitch but held himself back at great cost. She admired his restraint. To avoid a confrontation, one that Mitch seemed to be working toward, she stood. "Let's see if Lily needs a ride. Excuse us please."

They stood and Hannah hooked her arm in Cage's and pulled him along to where Lily sat at the far end of the table.

The strawberry blonde looked up as they approached.

"Hi Lily, Cage and I would like to offer you a ride back to town."

"Thank you, but the mayor has offered to escort me back. I guess you heard what happened to Pastor Marcus."

Lily patted the bench beside her and Hannah climbed over to take a seat while Cage talked to Carter and the mayor.

"So we're on first name basis with the parson are we?"

Lily tried to hide a huge grin behind the hand she pressed to her mouth. "Oh Hannah, he is the nicest man."

Hannah's heart swelled with joy. Lily was obviously in love. Her whole face shone as she spoke of 'her pastor.'

"I'm worried. He was stung many times. We must have disturbed a hive."

"Nellie will make sure he is looked after. Please try not to worry." Hannah laid a comforting hand on the young woman's arm.

Someone gripped her from behind and when she turned her head Bernice had her in a vice-like hug.

Hannah laughed and patted the arms that Bernice locked around her neck.

"Hello, come and sit with us."

As Bernice sat, Hannah looked to make sure Cage wasn't upset that her friends were monopolizing her time. But he was the center of a cluster of men. Mitch was at the far end of the table where another group had formed. Good, there was distance between the two men for now.

When she caught Cage's eye, he smiled and nodded and she settled in to enjoy a visit with the brides.

***

Mitch sat at the end of the table with his eyes on Hannah. She was everything he had ever wanted. He tried earlier to get Cage angry in the hope that Hannah would see him for the coward he was. But he just wouldn't fight.

It had always worked in the past. Since they were kids, he kept badgering him until Cage threw a punch or two, then he would refuse to continue fighting and allow Mitch to win. Mitch had become sheriff because many thought him the toughest man in the district.

How he would love to steal Hannah away right now. Leave Cage wondering where she had disappeared. But with all the cackling hens around her he decided to wait for his chance to spirit her away.

***

The picnic was winding down and Hannah placed dirty plates in a wooden crate. Cage and some of the other men took down the trestle table and benches and put them in a wagon.

Hannah smelled Mitch's overpowering aftershave before she turned to face him. She responded to his friendly smile with one of her own. Her heart sped as he stepped up to speak to her.

"You look lovely today, Hannah."

"Thank you." She caught sight of Cage out of the corner of her eye.

Cage had noticed them and was approaching with long deliberate strides.

"I'd like to invite you to supper to meet my parents at our ranch on Wednesday night."

Hannah remembered the friendly gentleman who had stopped by to inquire about Charlotte.

Cage was closing the distance with long stiff-legged strides.

"Yes, I'd like to have supper with your parents."

Cage scowled with a dangerous glint in his eyes. Hannah walked to meet him, cutting off his path to Mitch.

"What did he want?" Cage barked.

"I'll tell you on the way home. Let's go."

Cage took a rough grip on her elbow, his displeasure evident in the grasp he had on her arm.

He helped her onto the wagon and turned the horses, their hooves thundered as they left the yard more swiftly than was necessary.

Mitch tipped his hat to her in a final farewell.

***

Hannah held on tight to the bench seat of the wagon. Cage drove too fast as if he couldn't get away from the picnic fast enough. When she looked up at his face, she could see by the angry set of his jaw that he was in no mood to talk.

She understood that the trouble between the brothers went much deeper than jealousy. With God's help, she was determined to bring this family together and hopefully heal Cage's anger.

Mitch seemed to delight in trying to rile Cage into a confrontation. The problem was not something that would be easily resolved. Her place between the two of them didn't help. But she wanted to reconcile Cage with his father, Byron Campbell. If Cage knew his father, perhaps healing could take place.

Now that she understood his anger and hurt, she could see why he acted the way he did.

Underneath, there was a wonderful softhearted man. She had seen this side of him many times in the way he treated his mother and the animals on the farm. And lately, he treated her with that same regard.

A warm feeling spread through her as she thought of Cage without the anger and she was prompted to say, "Thank you Cage, for a wonderful day." She scooted closer to him on the bench and linked her arm in his. She leaned into his warm body. For a brief moment, he leaned over and she thought he might have kissed her hair.

"You're welcome."

She felt the tension leave him as his posture relaxed.

The cluster of trees and buildings that was Pine Creek came into view. Cage chose to drive through town. Hannah straightened and moved slightly on the bench to prevent tongues from wagging. She sat at a proper distance as they passed down the main street.

Something familiar caught Hannah's eye. It was an unusual coat that Harland's brother wore. It was a dark burnt orange color as if brown dye had washed out of the fabric.

Hannah felt the terror of waking up from a nightmare, with the monster from the dream still in the room. Her heart beat an erratic rhythm and threatened to burst out of her chest as she locked eyes with Harland's brother leaning against the mercantile wall. She perspired profusely and her hand flew to her mouth.

An evil half grin spread on the man's face turning it ugly.

He recognized her.

She buried her face in Cage's coat, but knew in her heart that it was too late.

Chapter Fifteen

By the day of the supper with the Campbell's, fear consumed Hannah. She sat by the bank of windows in the porch reading a book. She knew Cage and Charlotte had noticed how jumpy and out of sorts she had become, but she refused to mention why.

Harland was, no doubt, on his way. They were all safe until he arrived, but the anxiety was like a monster riding on her back. It was hard to think she was so exhausted, and her clothes had become loose. She kept lifting her eyes from the book to the laneway as she read. Bear barked at a rabbit and terror gripped her throat. She estimated she had a day left before Harland arrived.

When Mitch came to pick her up at three, she would find a way to tell him and see if he would protect her. She hoped to find a way so that law enforcement would protect her. She didn't expect her employers to be the ones to keep her safe. If all else failed she would run; take the train and bolt. The prospect saddened her. She didn't want to leave a job unfinished and she loved Charlotte.

She wasn't afraid to die. She knew death for a Christian meant security in the arms of her Saviour. But it was the method of death that she feared. She didn't want to think about slow and painful.

The memory of Harland as he killed his mother hit her full force. She fought the memory but it swirled into the nightmare that haunted her dreams.

A storm was brewing when she awoke that long ago morning in Boston. Angry snow-filled clouds gathered in the sky, and she wanted to arrive at her patient's home where she could weather the storm in comfort.

Hannah had arrived early that day at the elderly woman's home for her nursing shift. She hung her cape in the hall closet and her hands were red and raw when she pulled her gloves off and placed them in the pocket. She had twenty minutes before she was due to start.

The house was quiet but for the ticking of the hall clock as she climbed the mahogany stairs. The sound echoed eerie like a heartbeat in the stale air.

She reached the landing and was surprised to hear a shuffling noise and a mewling cry like that of a kitten from her patient, Evelyn's room.

She tiptoed across the floor until she stood in the doorway. Harland leaned over his mother's prone body holding a pillow down over her face. The poor woman's bony arms were flailing in a feeble attempt to get the pillow off her face. The image of the woman's arms flapping etched itself in Hannah's memory.

Hannah stood momentarily transfixed. The mewling stopped and the arms dropped to the bed. One hung over the edge like a lifeless doll. What she witnessed was horrifying.

"Harland, stop." Hannah screamed when her terror released its strangle hold.

She rushed forward and pulled at Harland's arm. He was twice her size and her efforts were pathetic as the monster leaned over his mother with all of his weight on the pillow.

"She's lingered long enough. I need the money _now_." His voice held a callus edge.

"No, please stop. Don't do this." Tears coursed down her cheeks as she desperately clawed at his arms.

Satisfied, he dropped the pillow. His arms bled where Hannah had scratched the skin away.

"Evelyn, Evie." Hannah called desperately and rushed to the bedside and lifted the pillow away. Vacant, hazel eyes stared heavenward. She shook her. No response.

She took the woman's pulse, but she was gone. Her chest ached as grief for her elderly patient overcame her. "Oh, Evie."

"Why did you do that?" She railed at Harland, swiping at tears that made a path down her cheeks. "She was already dying."

"I did it for us. We need the money." He gripped her forearms. "Now we can be together."

Together? Shock and horror washed over her as she realized this man had been harboring secret feelings for her and thought that now they could be a couple.

How had she never seen this?

Revulsion filled her and bile rose in her throat. She broke away.

"We need to tell the authorities." Her knees had become weak as she turned to go.

"What? No. Don't you understand I did it for us?" His expression changed when her intentions dawned on him, and he tried to regain his grasp on her.

She stumbled and scurried for the stairs. His bare feet slapped a rhythm on the hardwood floor of the upper landing as he chased her.

"Hannah, you can't tell anyone." He yelled as he followed her down the stairs.

"What you did is murder." She managed through her tears as she passed by the closet where her cape was stored. She ignored it; opened the heavy front door and kept going.

Snow covered the ground and she slipped and slid down the front steps to the sidewalk. The cold and wind hit her full force, ripping at her hair and skirts, but she barely felt it as she ran toward the street. She heard him curse as his bare feet hit the snow.

"I'll kill you, so help me I'll kill you." The monster yelled behind her. There was a thud, when she turned; he had landed hard at the bottom of the steps.

She knew he meant it.

Anyone that would kill his own mother . . . she shivered.

Harland's best friend was a cop. There would be no help from them. She had to get away. Find a way to leave Boston.

***

Cage came into the house at three o'clock. His brows knit together in a worried frown. "Your ride is here."

Hannah rose from where she had been sitting at the table. He clasped Hannah by the arms and waited until their eyes locked.

"You be careful with Mitch. I know I can't talk you out of this supper with the Campbell's. I've tried to for days. But I'm telling you, watch yourself with him."

His hands relaxed then and he whispered in her ear. "Come back safe."

A thrill ran through her when his warm breath caressed her cheek.

"I promise. I'll do what you told me if he is too bold."

Heat suffused her face when she remembered Cage's advice.

While in the barn the previous day, he warned her Mitch was known to be too bold with the ladies. He told her to knee Mitch in an unseemly place if she needed to get away from him. She knew Cage must be extremely worried otherwise he would never speak thus to a lady.

She bid Cage and his mother goodbye then walked out to Mitch who waited in the carriage. If this family were ever to heal, she needed to speak to Cage's father.

Mitch, dressed in his Sunday best, got down to help her into the buggy. He looked handsome in his good coat and a black Stetson.

"Hannah," he crooned when he placed a chaste kiss on her cheek.

She hoped Cage wasn't watching. It would only make matters worse.

The carriage rocked as Mitch climbed in beside her. He settled her under a warm lap robe. Hannah enjoyed the bright spring day, listening to

Mitch's chatter. She tried to work up the nerve to talk to him about Harland.

"Mitch I have a problem I need your help with." As he faced her, the smile he held left his eyes.

"What's that?"

"I saw a man in town on Saturday." Then a thought occurred to her. "Has anyone been asking for me in town?"

"Yes, there was a man asking for a woman of your description. I smelled a rat and was vague in my answer."

Fear choked her and she began to cry. Mitch stopped the team and placed an arm around her. Through her tears, she tried to tell Mitch the story.

"That was Harland's brother. I saw Harland kill his mother and he is on his way here to silence me."

Mitch's eyes widened in alarm, and he pulled her closer.

"I won't let him harm you, Hannah."

Her head lolled against his warm chest crushing the brim of her hat as she let the fear and tears go. As he held her tight in his arms, his strength reassured her.

When she had spent all of her tears, they continued on to the Campbell ranch discussing plans to keep her safe.

Hannah gasped when the Campbell farm came into view. The area of the yard was four times larger than Cage's. There were many more buildings, all in better repair. Bright white fences enclosed thoroughbred horses. A huge herd of cattle grazed off to the west.

Mitch stopped in front of the two-story, freshly painted house. Three herding dogs ran out to welcome them, barking out a wild greeting.

Hannah was struck by the contrast between Cage's and Mitch's upbringing. No wonder Cage's feelings ran deep.

"Do you like it?"

Hannah brightened her smile. "It's very nice."

She wondered if a girl like her could feel comfortable here, probably not.

The ornate oak door opened and Byron stepped outside and Hannah gave him a warm smile. He came down the steps and helped her from the buggy. His eyes welcomed her and his hands clasped hers in warm affection. Feelings of friendship collected in her chest and she squeezed his hands in return.

"Miss Wall, this is my wife." A small woman, dressed in the latest fashion with large puffed sleeves and a high collar, waited to make her acquaintance. Hannah offered her hand.

"Nice to meet you, Mrs. Campbell." Aloof, blue eyes appraised her, and Hannah shivered in discomfort.

Mitch drove the carriage to the barn and Byron, following his wife, escorted Hannah into the warm interior of the house.

Hannah took in the wainscoting in the entry hall, the Italian tile floor, and the redwood staircase leading to the upper floor. Beyond a polished railing, a dark skinned woman carried linens into one of the rooms.

They followed Mrs. Campbell to the parlor as her leather shoes clacked on the marble tiles.

Hannah's intake of breath was audible as she surveyed the room. A stone fireplace filled the end wall flanked by built-in bookshelves. A rich colorful oriental carpet covered the polished hardwood floor.

Byron seated her beside himself on a blue velvet sofa. Hannah had worked in many homes in Boston while caring for her patients, but none was ostentatious like this.

A servant entered with a tray and offered Hannah apple cider to sip while they waited for Mitch to join them.

A fit of nerves overcame Hannah while they spoke of pleasantries. In an effort to stop fidgeting, she laced her fingers together in her lap. Relief flooded her when Mitch returned having settled the horses in the barn.

Mrs. Campbell announced supper and Mitch escorted her into the dining room. Fear gripped her when she saw the richly appointed table. A snowy-white, lace tablecloth was set with three different crystal goblets and glasses. The light from a three-tiered chandelier made prisms through the glass and onto the lace. Three forks and several spoons flanked a gold-rimmed china plate.

She stiffened and Mitch whispered in her ear, "Just follow my lead."

Byron said grace and Hannah followed the others as they made their way through the many courses of the meal.

Over dessert, Mitch broached the subject of Harland. "Hannah needs our help, Dad. She witnessed a killing in Boston and the killer's brother has tracked her to Pine Creek."

Byron's fork thunked onto the lace tablecloth leaving a widening stain and Mrs. Campbell gasped. Bryon reached for Hannah's hand on the table beside him. "We won't let anything happen to you, dear."

Tears gathered in Hannah's eyes. She swallowed hard and tried to maintain control. Her throat stung with unshed tears.

"He promised to kill me to keep me from telling. He killed his mother for a great deal of money."

"You can stay here with us until this man is dealt with." Byron patted her hand and gave his wife a persuasive look.

Mrs. Campbell squirmed in her seat and patted her mouth with her napkin as if holding back the words she wanted to say.

"I can't possibly do that, but thank you for offering."

"Hannah listen, we can keep you safe here," Mitch pleaded.

"I need to be with Mrs. McCormack."

With the meal finished, Mrs. Campbell asked the servant to take their plates and bring coffee to the parlor.

Byron placed a reassuring arm around Hannah's shoulder and walked her to the great room where a fire crackled in the hearth. Hannah sat down and Mrs. Campbell offered a coffee from a large tray containing delicate bone china cups. She put cream and sugar in her coffee from a polished silver service.

Mrs. Campbell excused herself for a few minutes when a servant called her to the kitchen.

A few minutes later, a man came to the door asking for Mitch. He left to go to the front hall then came back to the doorway.

"I'm so sorry I have to leave. Problems in town. My father will make sure you are safe." He gave her a chaste kiss on the cheek and left.

Hannah prayed as she saw the opportunity she had hoped for when she agreed to this supper engagement.

"Mr. Campbell, would you be upset if I spoke to you for a moment about Micajah?"

The smile left Byron's face. "What about Cage?" He gave her a cold hard look.

Her resolve almost left her, but a voice inside prompted her to go on.

"You really need to heal the relationship with your son, sir."

"He hates me."

"He's angry, that's not the same as hate."

Byron moved away, deeper into the corner of the sofa. A closed thin-lipped look had taken over his face.

Mrs. Campbell chose that moment to re-enter the room.

"Please, think about it," Hannah whispered.

"What have you two decided?" Mitch's mother asked as she took a seat by the fire.

At first, Hannah didn't know what she meant, then realized that she was talking about her staying with them.

"Yes, Hannah, please stay here where we can protect you."

"Thank you for your kind offer, but I won't leave Charlotte."

Mrs. Campbell made a choking sound and said, "The young lady has made up her mind, Byron." A look of finality passed between them.

Chapter Sixteen

Cage paced back and forth by the long windows of the porch like a fenced stallion. Hannah should be home. <u>Now</u>. Evening had set in and light had faded. The clouds tinged with pink hovered over the laneway and still no carriage appeared.

The thought of Hannah with Mitch had eaten at Cage all day. Now it was a pain deep within his heart. He tortured himself with thoughts of what Mitch might do.

Visions of Hannah fighting his brother off kept popping into his head, his grubby hands on her, his slimy mouth all over hers and her ineffectual attempts to push him away. The scene played out in his head just as the one he had witnessed years ago behind the school when they were kids. He punched the wall in frustration and continued pacing.

Hannah was too precious to be sullied by the likes of Mitch. If she didn't arrive soon he would go and fetch her. He hoped he didn't have to go bust up the Campbell ranch. The few times he had rode there as a boy to catch a glimpse of his father, Mrs. Campbell had run him off.

His mother appeared in the doorway behind him. "Still no sign of Hannah, son?"

"No." He pulled her into a warm hug.

"Try not to worry. Byron will see no harm comes to her." She kissed his cheek. "I'm heading off to bed."

"I may have to go after her." She stopped and held the back of a nearby chair.

"All right, I'll be fine. Goodnight." She stopped at the door. "I'll keep her in my prayers."

He gave her a smile. "Thanks, mama."

Another hour passed. The moon rose in the dark sky, shedding a small amount of light onto the landscape.

Then Cage saw it. He jumped up and ran to the window. A light far off bounced as the buggy struggled over ruts and potholes. They say a man can see twenty miles across the prairie. Tonight, he was glad it was true. He breathed a sigh of relief. Hannah would soon be here.

The lantern attached to the front of the carriage continued to sway as it made slow progress toward him.

Anxious to see Hannah, Cage slipped his coat on and went to wait on the back porch. Bear, sleeping in the doorway of the barn, awakened to the sound of the buggy approaching. He barked and raced out to greet it.

Relief mixed with anxiety flooded through Cage. He paced the porch watching the light draw closer. It took everything in him not to race after his dog, his need to assure himself Hannah was all right strong.

Surprise jolted him as he recognized his father's gray head in the carriage beside Hannah. Not Mitch. His first thought was his brother had done something and Cage's hands balled into fists.

His second thought was that his father didn't recognize him as his son. He steeled his heart for his father's rejection.

When the buggy pulled up, he smiled at Hannah and offered his hand as she stepped down. He wanted to grab her into his embrace and assure himself she was in one piece but wouldn't in front of his father. Instead, he searched her eyes and saw no sign of distress.

"Thank you, sir, for the ride." Hannah's melodic voice sighed on the breeze.

"You're welcome."

Hannah proceeded into the house as Byron spoke. "Micajah, I need to speak to you about Hannah's safety."

"What did Mitch do?" Cage lashed out.

"Nothing." He gave a quizzical look. "It's a man named Harland she needs protection from."

Cage grabbed the strut on the buggy as he leaned in to hear what Byron had to say. Byron's baritone voice, so similar to his own, carried on the evening breeze as he explained to Cage the situation concerning Harland. He told him of Hannah's insistence that although she was in danger she refused to leave Charlotte.

"Why didn't she tell me?"

"She didn't want to burden you, her employer, with her safety." He pinned Cage with a serious stare. "I'm going to post riders on the road. They'll warn you if strangers approach. Mitch has no jurisdiction to arrest him. But I guarantee you, if he sneezes the wrong way, Mitch will arrest him or his kin."

"Thank you, I'll be ready here." Cage assured him.

Byron reached out to shake his hand as they finalized the plans. Cage hesitated briefly. It wasn't easy to let go of all the resentment he harbored against this man for so many years.

When he finally placed his work-worn hand into his father's bigger one, it surprised him how good it felt. Byron held it and said, "I sense the two of you boys are in competition for Hannah. I saw the way you looked at her. Either of you will be lucky to have her as your bride. She's a wonderful young woman."

"I know, sir." He pulled his hand away. "Thank you for bringing her home."

As the buggy turned and left the yard, many feelings gripped Cage. Elation, Hannah was home safe. Fear, he may not be able to protect her against a killer. Then a strange feeling of admiration for a father he barely knew. Then came the reminder of why he didn't know him.

He whistled for Bear, who had chased the carriage down the lane and said into the darkness, "I will die before I let that man hurt you, Hannah."

I'll keep her safe with Your help God.

***

Cage held the backdoor open for Hannah as she returned from the privy. He followed her into the kitchen.

"How was your supper with the Campbell's?"

"It was nice."

"Why didn't Mitch bring you home?" Cage asked, as he stoked the fire for the night.

"He was called away."

"Did he do anything to upset you?"

"No." He surveyed her face, but still found no sign she had a bad experience with Mitch.

She started towards his mother's room.

"Hannah why didn't you tell me about this man named Harland?"

She paused and gave him an apologetic smile. "Until now we've all been safe. I knew it would take Harland time to arrive here. The sheriff should be the one to deal with him."

She walked to his mother's room and stood in the doorway after checking on her.

A thought flashed across his mind like lighting on a warm prairie night. Did she think he was incapable of protecting her? Is that why she went to his brother? Or was it as she said, a problem for the sheriff?

He said goodnight, finished his nightly routine and went to the porch. He lit a lamp and spent time reading his bible and praying for guidance for when the time came to defend Hannah and his mother.

***

Hannah had been closing the window earlier when she heard Cage say, "*I will die before I let that man hurt you, Hannah.*" She knew he'd thought he was alone when he said it, but she had been standing behind the curtains and heard his declaration.

Now, while she lay in her room, she thought of the passion in his voice when he said it.

Could it be he cared for her? Truly cared?

His attitude had certainly changed toward her. Instead of an inconvenience he endured in order to have his mother home, he treated her as if he was glad to have her here and there was that look in his eye. The look said more than I just care.

Her thoughts turned to Mitch as she rolled to her side. She was fond of him at some level too.

Both men cared about her and both would try to keep her safe from Harland.

There it was, the horrible fear that gripped her soul and squeezed. She clenched her hands in the blankets and brought her knees up to her chest. She knew how a fox felt, hiding after the hunter has released the hounds.

***

The next afternoon Hannah and Cage worked on the flower garden by the back porch.

Charlotte rested reading a book in the enclosed front porch and watched the road.

Hannah enjoyed the new camaraderie she had with Cage. She appreciated his dedication to the land. When he wasn't hoeing the garden, he used a team of horses to break up the prairie sod.

He leaned over, took a large clod of earth in his hands, and squeezed it, sending a shower of clumps of rich prairie soil all over his work-worn boots.

"It's not ready for planting yet," he mumbled.

A horse whinnied in the corral alerting them to a rider's approach. Hannah recognized Byron as she straightened and leaned on her hoe.

"Micajah, Hannah, hello," he greeted, doffing his Stetson. "I have news."

Cage walked to where Byron had stopped and Hannah followed.

"Harland has been spotted in town. Mitch just got word to me and I came right over. The man with the orange coat is with him."

"That's his brother." Hannah stepped closer to Byron.

She trembled uncontrollably and Cage wrapped his arm around her shoulders.

She dropped her hoe and wrung her hands as she listened to Byron relate what the pair of men had been doing.

Fear rose in her throat and threatened to overwhelm her.

"They've asked about a woman of Hannah's description. Mitch has watched them, but they have done nothing he can arrest them for."

He beamed a reassuring smile down on Hannah. "I have two men stationed on the road leading to this farm. Should they approach, one of my men will ride here to warn you." His gaze strayed back to Cage. "He'll stay to help defend Hannah."

"I'll be ready." Cage assured him.

Hannah wiped at the tears that trickled down her cheeks. Byron alighted from his horse. "Hannah, try not to worry. We'll make sure no harm comes to you."

Could it be that the three of them would unite to protect her? Was God answering her prayers to reconcile this family? She hoped so.

Byron grasped her hand as he spoke. She stepped out of Cage's grasp and into Byron's fatherly embrace. The warm sheepskin of his open jacket smelled earthy. In the wonderful gentleman's hug, she allowed a feeling of safety to engulf her.

She knew Cage observed them. She hoped he would understand this man was worthy of his love and friendship.

As Byron released her and she stepped back with a drowning man's grip on his hand, she noticed the curtains on the nearby window slide back into place. She smiled to herself. Charlotte watched and perhaps understood the healing Hannah hoped would take place.

Byron mounted his horse, In a final farewell, reached down to shake hands with Cage.

"Be ready, boy."

Chapter Seventeen

The following days slipped by in a fear-filled haze. Harland was spotted twice and turned back at the road. Each time Hannah's anxiety became a living thing inside her. It threatened her appetite and denied her sleep.

In case she needed to leave in a hurry, Cage suggested she should learn to ride which made sense to her. The faster she could flee, the faster she drew the danger away from Charlotte. Today, Cage was determined to teach her, which shouldn't be a problem except her fear of the huge animal.

"Talk to her Hannah." He held the large head still by the halter.

She timidly patted the horse's soft warm muzzle. She loved horses. Even admired them from a distance. She just needed to get used to their massive size when she stood next to them.

She stroked the horse's neck and whispered.

The large head tossed and Hannah jumped back.

"It's all right," he said steadying the horse. " When she nods like that she's letting you know she likes you."

"I like her, too. I need to get over the difference in our size."

Cage stood beside her stroking the horse's neck. The cow and barn odor on his clothes no longer bothered her. After milking Bessy every evening, those scents were familiar and no longer repugnant.

His chest brushed her shoulder causing her heartbeat to become erratic.

"Are you ready to sit in the saddle?" His breath whispered along her neck sending a shiver through her spine.

She nodded.

Cage threaded his fingers together and held them creating a cup so she could mount the horse. "Grasp the horn and pull yourself up as I lift. Ready? One, two, three."

She swung her free leg over the horse's back and sat astride feeling far too high off the ground. Her fear of heights caused her to squeeze her knees tight on the animal's flanks and take a death grip on the saddle horn. Her skirt had hiked up and she struggled to cover her exposed legs with one hand.

Cage patiently waited to hand her the reins. "She's not going to buck you off."

He adjusted her skirt pulling it further down.

"When the time comes, you may have to ride bare back." Hannah met his eyes and swallowed hard. "She's so big. I'm too far off the ground."

Cage smiled. "I didn't know you're afraid of heights."

She gave him, what she hoped, was a brave smile.

"Just sit for a moment and give your brain time to adjust to your distance from the ground."

Cage gave her instructions on how to handle the horse. When he was finished, she realized her grip had relaxed on the saddle horn and she no longer felt the height intolerable.

A new sense overtook her as Cage walked the horse slowly around the yard. He allowed her to get used to the swaying of the animal's back. She focused on his profile as he led her horse and a fondness for this man infused her. Something she never would have expected when she first met him.

When he stopped and handed her the reins, her fingers brushed the calluses on his strong hands. It sent tingles loose within her. She looked his way but he stepped away to mount his own horse. She noticed a bulge under his shirt at the small of his back. Her brows furrowed then relaxed. He'd hidden a handgun in the waistband of his denim pants.

Fear shot through her stealing her breath. Then she realized how determined he was to keep her safe. Gratitude and love filled her chest with an aching sweetness.

They rode together around the perimeter of the yard. As they came around the west side, she spied Byron in the distance. He stopped, sitting quietly on his horse. Surprised to see him, grateful he was there, Hannah waved and beckoned. Byron doffed his hat but refused to ride in.

What a wonderful man to take time out of his busy day to keep me safe.

After twenty minutes, Cage led her into the dark interior of the barn. When she dismounted, Cage held her by the waist, her lips inches from his. Their eyes locked. She looked deep into the dark eyes fixed on her and waited, hoping for a kiss.

He searched her face for something, an answer maybe. She put her hands through his black tousled hair and pulled his face closer.

Taking her signal, Cage pulled her into a kiss. All of the love available in her heart poured into her lips as she kissed him back.

He lowered her feet to the ground releasing her. She stood on tiptoes pulling his head down for another one. She abandoned herself to the beauty of the loving feelings she had for this man and allowed him to deepen the kiss to another level. This time when he released her, her head spun and her toes curled.

"You feel it, too?" Cage asked in a whisper.

"Yes. Yes, I do."

"Oh, Hannah." He pulled her into an embrace. "I don't deserve you."

"You're all I need." She whispered into his shirt.

"Well, isn't this just the most blissful scene?" A familiar male voice spoke from the shadows of the stall nearest the door.

Harland's brother!

Chapter Eighteen

Startled by the strange voice, Cage gasped then tried to see into the stall nearest to the door. Disturbed dust motes danced in the sunlight streaming in the large open barn door.

The person who spoke must have just entered.

Hannah stood beside him rooted to the spot clutching her chest.

"Who's there?" He tried to get a fix on the man.

Light glinted off metal.

A gun!

He was in the first stall his form concealed in the dark.

Cage stepped in front of Hannah to shield her. His pulse pounded in his ears and fear rose in a wave, making it hard for him to think. The man clearly had the drop on him. To pull out his own gun would force the man to use his. Hannah could be hurt, killed or if Cage went down, kidnapped.

Promises from the Bible filtered through his mind.

Let not your heart be troubled. Believe also in Me. When you walk in the shadow of death fear no evil.

Hannah spoke from behind him. "It's Harland's brother, Harold."

A figure in a rusty-orange coat stepped out of the dark. The man's face hidden in the shadows made him appear like a phantom. The gun pointed directly at Cage's chest. The man wore an old slouch hat pulled low over his eyes. His chin held several days' growth of gray beard.

Cage wanted to gauge the man's eyes but couldn't see them, not a good position to be in, in a gunfight.

Cage would watch and his eyes would signal when he was about to shoot his gun. His friend Nicholai, the blacksmith, had taught Cage that.

"What do you want?" Cage watched the gun quiver.

"Harland wants a word with his woman."

"I'm not his woman." Cage felt Hannah shift behind him.

"Tie him up." Harold growled and tossed her a rope from a peg on the wall.

She let it fall to the ground at her feet.

"Pick it up and do as I say or he gets a hole in um."

Before Cage could stop her, Hannah snatched the gun from his waistband and stepped out with the pistol pointed at

Harold. Cage's heart lodged in a painful mass in his throat as the two faced off, both with a gun. The hand holding the gun pointed at Hannah trembled. Cage held his breath. The man was clearly not used to a gun and it could easily go off at any moment. He scrambled for a safe way to diffuse the situation.

"Drop the gun, or lover boy gets a load of lead." His voice quivered. He spit a sludgy mass of tobacco into the dirt.

Seconds ticked by endlessly.

Cage's mind whirled as he tried to think of a safe way to disarm Harold. The man was nervous and the gun could easily go off.

Hannah still stood slightly behind him. He feared any movement on his part could cause one of them to start firing with disastrous results.

What should he do?

A loud thud echoed in the still air.

Hannah had dropped the gun. "Please don't hurt him. It's me you want."

"Tie him to that post," Harold growled.

Afraid the man would shoot Hannah if he rushed him for the gun, Cage allowed himself to be tied. He would have to let Harold take her and trust Bryon would see them leaving and save her.

As Hannah tied him to the post, the abrasive twine scratched at his wrists. He prayed Byron was still outside. He flicked Hannah a look of reassurance as she finished binding him. He mouthed the word "Byron".

She nodded.

Hannah's eyes were as big as dinner plates and her hands shook as she tried to tie the cord.

The fear in her eyes ripped at his heart. He had to depend on his father now, the heavenly one and the earthly one, to keep her safe.

Harold checked to make sure the rope was secure gagged Cage's mouth with a bandana then led Hannah away.

He struggled against the rough cord to free his hands. It didn't give. Harold had pulled the knots tight.

He listened for sounds of gunshots in the hope Byron stopped them. The only sound came from the prairie wind and horses stamping in the corral.

All Cage could thing of was Harland would probably kill Hannah when she reached him. He had to get loose. He twisted against the twine. He could feel it dig into his flesh but it wouldn't give.

Desperate to get loose, he kicked in frustration.

He banged his heel on something metal lying behind him in the dirt. An old discarded shovel lay within his boot's reach. His spur clinked on the metal sending metallic sounds ringing. He hoped Byron was close enough to hear. He varied them to draw attention to the barn.

This has to work. Please Lord.

Minutes later, Byron appeared in the doorway.

"Micajah, what happened?" Byron hurried to untie him.

"Harland's brother, has Hannah. Did you see them leave?"

"No. They must have skirted around the barn where I wouldn't see them." He worked behind Cage to unravel the knots.

"I'll tell my mother what's happened. See if you can pick up the trail."

"All right." Byron rushed out into the bright sunlight beyond the barn door.

"Wait for me ah . . . Byron."

"Of course."

Cage found his mother in the kitchen chopping vegetables for supper.

In an effort to shield his mother, Cage said, "Mama, Hannah's missing. Byron and I are riding out to bring her back."

Charlotte's face drained of color, the knife in her hand suspended in mid-air, as her mouth dropped open. "Please, find her."

"I will." Cage gave her a quick kiss on the forehead.

"I'll pray, my son."

She followed him to the door. He turned on the porch and hugged her. Her sweet scent calmed him. "Try not to worry," he whispered in her ear.

Bryon sat astride his horse holding Cage's reins. He nodded to Charlotte as Cage mounted.

"The trail is out behind the barn." He led the way to where the hoof marks led across the prairie. The sparse new spring grass showed a trampled path that was easy to follow.

We'll catch him.

The path wound around in a long circle that headed back to the road that led into town.

They tracked the horses into town where they lost the trail. There were far too many hoof prints in the dirt to distinguish one particular set. Pain filled Cage's chest when it became evident Harold had given them the slip. Hopelessness wrapped itself around his heart and squeezed. He fought hard to swallow the tears that gathered and threatened to embarrass him.

Bryon went straight to Mitch's office. After a slow dismount, he handed his reins to Cage who waited on his horse. Cage's stubborn pride would not allow him to talk to Mitch. He wished he didn't need Mitch's help, but it was clear if they were to find Hannah, they would all have to work together.

He leaned over, burying his face in his horse's mane and prayed. "Please Lord, help me put my feelings toward these men aside so we can find Hannah. Please keep her safe. Send Your angels to protect her."

When he raised his head, he realized he had not thought of angels since he was a child. He forgot the power of God. A new hope bloomed in his chest and peace settled over him. He knew if he trusted God they would find Hannah.

Mitch, Byron and two other men emerged from the sheriff's office. Cage's fingers tightened into fists around the reins in his hands, his nails biting into his palms. He fought to let go of the old bitter feelings that erupted in him at the sight of Mitch. It galled him when Mitch took control of the search party and gave orders.

Typical Mitch, all puffed up and self important.

They searched for hours and found no sign of Hannah. Finally gathering back at the sheriff's office.

"Thanks men. We'll meet back here at first light." Mitch dismounted and tied his horse to the hitching rail.

Tired and discouraged, Cage just wanted to go home.

Byron, still mounted beside Cage said, "Come, I'll buy your supper."

Exhausted, Cage turned his horse to follow his dad to the hotel where Nellie would have coffee. He would need the coffee. He still had an hour's ride home in the dark.

Seated at a table for two across from his dad, Cage ordered coffee and Byron ordered the special that night, venison stew.

"Come on now, you'll need energy for the search tomorrow."

"I just can't til we find Hannah."

"Try not to worry. We'll find her." Byron eyed him from under knit brows.

"I'm afraid they're long gone. Not just holding her at an abandoned homestead as Mitch seems to think."

"We'll gather more men and widen the search tomorrow. Are you sure you won't stay in town?"

"No, I have to go home for mother. I'll move her here to the hotel while we search. I honestly thought we would find them today. I pray she's still alive."

Byron reached across the table and patted Cage's hand.

"We'll find her."

A soul numbing fear gripped him and he wondered how he could go on breathing. He wanted to put on sackcloth and ashes the way men did in the bible. If he thought it would do any good, he would have. Instead, he spent the entire ride home praying and

crying out to God to please keep Hannah safe.
Please let her be alive when we find her Lord.

Chapter Nineteen

The citizens of Pine Creek were wonderful during this time. Nellie took Cage's mama under her wing. Charlotte helped in the kitchen of the hotel preparing food and set up tables in the dining room.

The grooms took time away from courting the brides to help in the search.

Byron had one of his hired men stay at Cage's ranch to look after the crops, horses and cattle.

The brides pitched in to prepare and serve food for the searchers when they arrived weary and disgruntled after dark each night.

Cage appreciated every act of kindness.

Days of searching slipped by. They checked nearby towns but no one had seen Hannah or her captors. No travellers who stopped in Pine Creek had remembered encountering them. The days of looking fell into a routine. Cage and his mother now stayed at the hotel. When the men arrived back there long after dark, Charlotte would join them and have a cup of tea as they ate. Cage picked at the food on his plate and he had begun to lose weight. He became more disheartened with each passing day.

"Cage we may have to stop the search. She may already be dead." Mitch told him from across the table one night.

Cage hated him for putting a voice to what rung in his own ears for the last few days. In his heart, he knew Mitch was right.

Could it be over? Was she gone?

"I thought I'd feel it if she was dead." Cage mumbled, then realized he had spoken aloud. Tears threatened at the back of his throat.

"You really love her," Mitch whispered.

"Yeah, I do." Cage rose, scraping his chair he almost knocked it over in his haste.

He had to leave now before he embarrassed himself with the grief that gathered in his eyes.

He left the hotel and wandered to the edge of town. He stumbled at times, blinded. He thought his chest might explode with the pain encased inside.

He missed her and longed for her so much.

"Hannah, where are you?" he called into the wind. "Are you dead and I just don't feel it?"

The wind blew across his face cutting deep into his pain but refused to give the answer he so wanted.

The last moments he spent with her played in the corridors of his mind. They were so wonderful. So precious. Her lips so soft, so sweet.

He brought his hand to his forehead in frustration. He tortured himself with thoughts of her.

"Heavenly Father, I've never asked for rain for my crops or a good harvest but Lord I need Hannah. You know I don't want to go on without her. Only You know if she is alive or dead. I pray she's still safe but if not, please let us find her and bury her. Take away my pain."

He caved in to his grief as the realization set in. He might never see her again.

***

After weeks had passed, Mitch stood before the crowd in the hotel dining room.

"Folks, can I have your attention?"

Cage's heart dropped and he grabbed his mother's veined, wrinkled hand beside him on the table.

The chatter in the room stopped as all eyes fixed on Mitch. "I want to thank all of you for the sacrifices you've made in the weeks we've been hunting for Hannah." His Adam's apple bobbed as he swallowed hard and Cage noticed his knuckles whitened on the back of the chair he held.

"We'll end the search tonight until further notice. Please keep your eyes and ears peeled for any sign of her."

There were audible gasps from several of the women in the room. Bernice broke down and some of the brides began to cry. Charlotte dabbed at her eyes with a hanky she carried.

A sense of hopelessness washed over Cage. He felt like a wet rag that had just come through the scrub board.

"Pack up in the morning, Mama. We'll leave for home at noon."

Tears filled his eyes and his chair tipped over as he rushed from the room. Mitch caught up to him near the bushes at the side of the hotel. Cage heard him approach and hastily swiped at the tears on his cheeks.

"I'm so sorry Cage. I know now, how much you love her."

"I can't believe she's dead. I thought I would feel it."

Cage pounded his chest spreading the pain deeper.

"I should have done more." Mitch laid a hand on his shoulder.

"It's all right. You and your dad have been great. I couldn't have asked for more."

Mitch looked him in the eye, patted him on the shoulder and said, "He's your dad too, Cage."

Cage's eyes involuntarily widened in complete surprise. The time they spent together in the last weeks had changed them, he marveled.

"Thanks, Mitch," he whispered as pesky tears threatened to fill his eyes again.

Byron found both of his boys huddled in the shadows. "You fellas all right?"

"He thinks we're still fighting," Mitch whispered. He slipped an arm around Cage's shoulders. "We're fine Dad." He said louder.

"All we can do is wait, boys." Byron joined them in the shadows.

"Right," said Cage and blew out a long breath.

In the midst of this tragedy, a few good things had developed. The hunt and concern for Hannah had united the family. Cage noticed a change in Mitch, as well. He no longer taunted him . Anger was no longer a living thing just under the surface.

A weight that he hadn't realised he carried had lifted out of his chest and off of his shoulders.

***

A month went by with no news. Cage and his mother limped along, managing day by day to exist. Easter had come and they attended the service but their hearts weren't in it. Cage found none of the usual enjoyment in the yearly gathering of friends. Cage sat stoic and waited for the service to end.

Afterward they gathered outside, the brides were all atwitter. A bride named Constance announced she was soon to be married. It only caused Cage's chest to tighten and the pain that dwelled permanently there to spread. In these dark days, he found it hard to cling to God's word and His promises. But deep down he believed God knew best. He sees the tapestry of life from both sides.

As he guided the wagon home after the service, he remembered something his mama had shown him long ago.

"Mama tell me again about the tapestry."

"The tapestry?" She twisted toward him, giving him her full attention.

"It was an illustration you told me a long time ago about the difference between the way we see the world and our lives and the way God sees it."

"Yes, my needlepoint, of course." Her face brightened.

"God sees our life from the side of the canvas with the perfect stitches I made, and the beautiful picture it was becoming." she told him. Then she had turned the tapestry over and showed him the underside. The threads snarled together where she had woven them in to keep them from unravelling. "I had to do this so the beautiful picture wouldn't fall apart over time.

"This messy side is how we see our life. All messed up with no purpose, not very pretty, making no sense at all.

"We need to remember God has a plan for our life, and if we follow His plan and not our own. Our life will become something beautiful. Just like the perfect picture the tapestry becomes."

***

God knows best, but to live it became harder as each day passed. He missed Hannah's sweet nature, the soft voice she used when she spoke to his mother. He even missed her 'locking' the doors at night, and sneaking food out to Bear. It amazed him that the birds still sang and the sun still rose every morning. Didn't they know it was the end of his world? Why wasn't the rest of the world as dark and lonely as he felt?

He put hay out for the horses and was lost in the daydream of kissing Hannah when Bear began to bark and make a fuss.

When he walked out to the front yard, Mitch rode in.

"Mount up, Cage. We've spotted her."

"What? She's alive?" A feeling akin to panic, an overwhelming emotion, hit him full in the chest.

"Yes, go." Mitch gestured to the barn.

"Tell my mama." Cage hollered over his shoulder as he ran.

Anxiety squeezed his chest as he raced into the barn. He grabbed his saddle and tack and brought it out to the corral. It would have made more sense just to take the horse out of the corral into the barn, but he was far too excited to think logically. His heart pounded and his hands shook as he hurried.

"Your mom is all right with you leaving. Dad will send a man to look after things." Mitch steadied the horse as Cage tried to stop shaking to tighten the cinches.

"Where did they find her?"

"A stranger came through town and I questioned him as usual. He claims Harland and his brother are holding her a day's ride from here in an old abandoned soddie."

"He's sure she's still alive?" Cage asked as they both mounted.

"Yeah, Harland told the guy she was his wife."

Cage's fists balled into tight knots. His chest burned with anger.

Charlotte came out of the house with a gunny sac full of food for the trip.

"Thanks, Mama. Pray," he whispered as he took the sack and tied it to his saddle horn.

"We'll head to Dad's ranch." Mitch turned his horse.

As he spurred his horse to a gallop, Cage prayed for Hannah. He prayed for her safety. He prayed for strength. Most of all, he prayed she wasn't married to Harland.

Anger, hope, elation and fear took turns churning inside him as they raced across the prairie. He begged God Hannah was all right.

Chapter Twenty

Hannah peeled vegetables into a large pot. Harland had gone out to hunt rabbits or deer. Harold, his brother, sat outside by the fire keeping watch over her. She waited for a way to escape but so far, none had come.

They were living a primitive life in a small structure made of blocks of prairie sod cut out of the grassy ground and piled one on top of the other like bricks. She heard earlier settlers had called them soddies and lived in them until they could haul in wood for a more habitable home.

Hannah found the one room building cool in the heat of the day and it held the warmth of a small fire at night.

She stopped her potato peeling to scratch at her head. Because the hut and its roof were made of dirt, sand sifted down onto everything making her feel dirty and itchy.

"Harold ,Harold come quick," she screeched jumping up from the makeshift table.

"What now?"

She backed away pointing to the offending bug.

"Come on lady. What do I look like? Your royal servant or something. It's just a little centipede minding his own business."

"Please Harold, take it away." She begged from her position against the wall.

"All right but this is the last time today."

He scurried out the door dangling the wiggly creature.

She checked the area carefully before sitting down to finish her task. As she peeled the last potato, she thought about what a relief it was to have Harland gone for a while. Although he hadn't forced himself on her in a sexual way, he was determined to win her over. That's why he had her here in the middle of nowhere. Isolated, so there was no escape and she had to depend on him for everything. He thought if he kissed her and held her, he could break her down.

She knew she should be grateful he hadn't killed her. Because of his obsession, convinced that he loved her, he wanted her alive. He repulsed her by his need to constantly kiss, touch and hug her. But because it kept her alive, waiting to be rescued, she tried not to show how much it sickened her.

All she could think of was Cage.

She daydreamed about him constantly and prayed he would find her. She prayed he wouldn't give up. Even now, she thought of how much he had changed since she first met him. Resolving things with his dad would heal him. In recent days, before the kidnapping, he showed a warmer, gentler side that pleased her.

She thought of his kiss and how alive it had made her feel. Every nerve wanting to be touched, a physical response to the loving feelings they had for one another.

She had no expectations of finding love when she had arrived in Pine Creek, but love had found her and now Harland wanted to destroy that and take it all away.

She had tried several times to get away, but with only the open prairie to escape to, any attempt became fruitless. They noticed right away when she tried running across the grassy expanse.

She was glad Cage had briefly taught her to ride. If she were ever to get away, it would have to be by horseback. She kept hope alive, thinking she could someday grab a horse and go. Praying she wouldn't fall off. But Harold slept each night right by the door while Harland insisted she sleep next to him on a pallet in one corner.

Another thing she worried about was even if she did escape and make her way back to Cage. He might not want her after she had spent time alone with two men. The women in town might shun her now too, thinking the men had sullied her.

Thankfully, that hadn't happened. Harland insisted on waiting until she came to him voluntarily.

She did not intend to have that happen. Him kissing her forehead made her shudder.

The sound of a horse approaching brought her out of her reverie, and she carried the large pot outside so that Harold could place it over the fire. Harland was back.

***

While the three men on horseback crossed the prairie together, Cage wondered why Mitch refused to bring extra men with him.

Mitch, was clearly in charge and could have brought every man on the Campbell ranch with him. But at the last minute, he decided only the three of them would go. This was not the way Cage would have done things and he squeezed the reins tighter in silent protest. Was Mitch trying to prove something to their father? Prove he was the big hero?

After riding all day at nightfall, they spotted the campfire at the soddie. Cage's heart quickened when he realized Hannah was now within reach.

They tethered their horses about a mile from the soddie at a copse of trees by a natural pond.

"Why can't we just rush them now?" Cage refused to dismount.

"No Cage, we'll rush in at first light." Mitch pulled jerky out of his saddlebag.

Cage's first reaction was to ride in guns blazing. But that would put Hannah in danger so he had to rein in his feelings and try to think with a clear head. Mitch was right.

"What if they leave?" He dismounted angrily.

"After I eat and rest for a bit. I'll ride over to the far side. I know what I'm doing, Cage."

For a moment, Cage heard the voice of that smart aleck schoolboy again, and his blood boiled. He ground his mouth shut and shoved his fists in his pockets.

He looked to Byron, but he seemed fine with having Mitch in charge. He had settled his back against a tree and crunched on an apple.

Clearly overruled, Cage tried to settle himself to wait for dawn.

The night crawled by. Cage was certain he saw a glimpse of Hannah's blue dress in the firelight once. He lay on his belly in the grass until the wee hours watching the campfire outside the soddie. As the hours passed, the flames became smaller until only the glow of embers was visible. Cage's arms became stiff and his hands went to sleep he stayed in one position so long.

Mitch awoke and readied himself and his horse to circle around to the far side.

"Mitch, we really need to stay together."

"No Cage, I know what I'm doing."

Disgusted, Cage watched Mitch leave, losing sight of him in the dark night. He couldn't just rush in by himself. But he wanted to.

Unable to sleep, Cage went over some 'what ifs.'

What if Hannah were hurt when they tried to rescue her?

What if Harland just shot her the moment he saw them coming?

Fear for Hannah tore at his chest and filled it with pain.

His stomach roiled in agony.

A coyote howled in the distance and he flinched. Byron stirred nearby and softly snored.

Please be with Hannah, Lord. Whatever happens in the morning, please keep her safe. He prayed on until he felt a peace settle over him.

Cage listened to the birds chirp back and forth to one another as they did every morning just as dawn broke. Their world would go on as usual. He feared his life would never be worth living if they didn't bring Hannah home safe.

Cage woke Byron, checked his saddle, and cinched it tight.

He worried about the flaw in Mitch's plan to come in from the far side. How were they going to coordinate their attack? He and Byron had no idea when Mitch would strike. He would get Hannah killed!

Realization washed over him and caused his fists to clench. Mitch planned to rush in on his own and take all the glory.

Oh, this is so typical of Mitch. A glory seeker who wanted to be the big hero.

That was fine if it worked, but without Byron and Cage's help, he could put Hannah at risk.

"Come on Byron, we need to get over to where Mitch is before he does something stupid."

"What?"

"All three of us need to ride in together. His plan could get himself or Hannah killed."

"We better get over there." Byron rolled up his bedroll.

They mounted up and began the long circuitous ride to where Mitch was hiding on the far side.

Cage prayed Mitch wouldn't try his ill conceived plan before he and Byron found him.

When they were about half way to the other side, skirting far from the soddie to stay hidden, a ruckus erupted at the dirt building.

Cage's heart dropped.

He felt like a man walking across a frozen lake and just heard the ice crack beneath him. The bottom was about to fall out from under him.

Chapter Twenty One

Hannah lay slumbering in a sleep world with shadows and strange grotesque men that resembled Harland and his brother. She was wedged between Harland and the earthen wall of the soddie. She faced the wall preferring the earthy smell to that of the musky smell of Harland. Neither man had bathed since their arrival. Startled awake she wondered what was happening.

The fearful emotions of the dream became panic as she awoke to sounds of a scuffle in the doorway.

Harold and Harland both confronted someone.

"Drop the gun, now." Harland's voice echoed in the small space.

Unable to see in the predawn dark, Hannah's chest squeezed in painful fear. Who was there and what was happening?

She sat up on the pallet and shivered in the cold. She pulled a blanket around her and stood up, squinting unable to see.

"Drop yours." She heard Mitch's familiar deep voice.

Relief flooded through her and her heart raced. In her sleepy mind the thought finally came, he had arrived to rescue her.

A shadow outside, she could barely make out, lunged forward. She could make out Harland's tall silhouette on top of Mitch's burly form, their arms and legs flailing as they scuffled in the dirt. Fear for Mitch's safety gripped her.

"Get up both of you." Harold had found the shotgun in the pitch black of the hut and pointed it at Mitch. The two men scrambled to their feet.

"Get a fire started, Harold, and we'll decide what to do with this worthless dog." Harold handed the gun to Harland and went to do his bidding.

Hannah's blood ran cold. She remembered how easily he had snuffed out his mother's life.

Help us Lord. Please be with us.

She threw off the worn shirt of Harold's she wore at night, dressed, and followed the men outside.

What will we do now, Lord?

Mitch's face showed relief when Hannah stood unharmed in the doorway. She gave him a grateful smile. Harold had a fire of kindling started and Harland was busy tying Mitch's hands behind his back.

Hannah wondered if Mitch was alone, or if he had brought men with him. She peered into the darkness but could see nothing.

"Make us some coffee, Hannah." Harland barked from the far side of the fire. "Go get your gun, Harold."

As she bent down taking on the familiar task, she pondered if she could use the boiling water to get herself and Mitch free. Knowing she would have to disable both brothers at once, it wasn't likely to work. With Mitch's hands tied, he wouldn't be much help even if she could manage to scald one of the brothers.

Her mind whirled as she tried to stay focused and think. It was a relief Mitch was there. At least she wasn't alone.

The horizon in the distance stained pink as the dawn broke, casting a strange hue on things with more cerise light. As she stooped to put more fuel on to the fire, Byron and Cage stepped into the firelight.

She gasped. *Cage.*

Mitch rose beside them from the ground where he sat. All three Campbell men faced Hannah's captors. Harold had returned with his pistol. Of the five men, all but Mitch had guns and drew down on one another.

Hannah dropped the buffalo chips in her hands and held her breath. Her racing heart thundered in her ears.

A wicked smirk took over Harland's face. "You boys want to die today? Who wants to go first?"

She wobbled and her vision blurred. Hannah struggled not to faint as the impact of his words hit home.

To her right stood Mitch, then Cage and Byron furthest from her. To her left Harland stood ready to shoot either Cage or Mitch. Harold aimed straight at Byron. She inched her way toward Cage, afraid Harland might grab her and change the odds of the situation. She knew the Campbell men would drop their weapons if Harland threatened her.

Seconds ticked by as the men sized up one another. Hannah kept her eyes averted, unwilling to make eye contact in case she distracted them and gunfire erupted.

She prayed harder hoping God would intervene.

A hand reached out and before she could move, she was in Harland's grasp. She had been distracted and now he had her.

"Drop your weapons, boys."

Just the thing she wanted to avoid, she had let happen.

As Harland clutched her, his bony fingers digging in, her heart filled with self-loathing.

Two guns thumped into the dirt. One landed against the stones that circled the hot campfire.

"Tie them up." Harland told his brother.

Harold came from the soddie moments later and tied Byron's hands first, leaving Cage 'til last.

Harland released Hannah to watch that Byron or Cage didn't try anything.

"Get me a coffee, woman, while I decide what to do with this bunch."

Glad to be out of Harland's grasp, Hannah obeyed. When she picked up the coffee, a gunshot went off. Scared senseless, she flung the coffee pot across the fire straight at Harold.

Byron saw it coming and stumbled back to avoid the boiling hot liquid. Harold took it full on the chest and howled in agony.

Hannah was certain Harland would shoot. She flung herself past Mitch, in front of Cage.

*

Cage's heart dropped into his stomach when Hannah stepped into the line of fire. If Harland fired now, she would be dead.

Only seconds passed, but to Cage they ticked by endlessly. If a bullet passed into Hannah at this distance, she would die instantly. Gone forever, the woman he loved. Gone forever, the person who had changed his life. The person who had given him a relationship with his father. Gone forever, the future he dreamed of with Hannah as his bride.

Cage clasped her shoulders and set her aside out of harms way. Then he grabbed the gun that rested against the hot stones of the fire. The metal burned his flesh, but he refused to drop it. Pain shot through his hand and up his arm but he held on.

"Drop the gun, now." His thumb burned as he cocked the gun.

Harland sidetracked had lowered his gun. He dropped the gun and raised his hands in defeat.

Byron had Harold pinned to the ground with one booted heel. He writhed in agony unable to muster the strength to get away. His gun lay in the dirt a safe distance away.

Hannah untied Mitch and he tied Harland.

Cage hugged Hannah to him. He bent to kiss her cherished face. She was safe and she clung to him like a drowning victim to a lifeline.

"Oh Cage." Was all she said as tears of joy coursed down her face.

"I love you, you're safe now."

They tidied the site, hitched the wagon Harland had used to haul supplies while Byron retrieved the horses from where he and Cage had hobbled them.

Cage drove the wagon with Hannah's small form beside him, the prisoners in the back. Mitch and Byron followed on horseback.

Hannah pressed herself tightly to his side. Hannah's warmth infused him. She had tucked herself up under his shoulder. He hugged her close with his free arm. She fit perfectly.

She was his now. Mitch would bow out gracefully. He had alluded to that earlier. Cage relaxed enjoying the sunny day.

"You all right?"

"Yes, I'm fine, now." She hugged his arm pressing her cheek into his coat. All was well and he looked forward to sharing the good news with those who waited back at Pine Creek.

Chapter Twenty Two

A sense of relief and excitement sprang from Hannah's heart as they crossed mile after mile of prairie.

She was content now, knowing Cage was the one. It was a wondrous feeling to know that she would live out her life with what could only be described as her soul mate, Cage. Yes, he was abrasive and cantankerous at first, not exactly lovable. Hannah smiled. But with God's help, and through prayer, she had witnessed a metamorphosis. Oh, he still had his rough edges. She wasn't fooled. Life with him would hold many challenges but she trusted God to see them through the rough patches.

When the town came into view a few miles in the distance, she became anxious to see Charlotte. She grinned. Even one of Bernice's bear hugs would be welcome today.

When the wagon pulled up, people poured out of the hotel and the surrounding stores. Hannah was certain the entire town knew of her rescue and as word spread more people gathered to welcome her home.

As the mayor helped her from the wagon, the crowd cheered and embarrassment stained her cheeks.

"Welcome back, young lady." The mayor's voice betrayed the emotion he felt.

"Thank you, Mayor. It's good to be back."

Bernice was next, nearly knocking the other brides off the steps in her haste.

She crushed Hannah into the bear hug Hannah knew would come.

"I was so worried about you."

"I'm fine, Bernice."

"We have so much to catch up on. I'm engaged to Carter now."

She flashed a pretty locket under Hannah's nose. Hannah smiled at Bernice's enthusiasm. She took hold of it and held it out where she could focus on it properly.

"Oh Bernice, congratulations. It's beautiful." Her heart burst for the bride that had become dear to her.

"Lily's married to the preacher and Constance is married now."

"Oh my, I have a lot of catching up to do."

Bernice squeezed her again then moved aside to let Charlotte step forward.

Tears filled Hannah's eyes as she embraced Charlotte and held her tight.

It was as if she were back in her own mother's arms. It felt so wonderful.

"I missed you, dear."

"I missed you, too."

"How have you been?" Hannah pulled back to take a good look and assess her patient. Charlotte's cheeks were wet with tears and she brushed them away.

"I've been fine, dear. Worried sick over you. But I'm getting stronger every day. Nellie has let me help while I stayed here at the hotel and we continued my therapy as best we could."

Hannah spotted Nellie then in the crowd standing on the porch and flashed her a grateful smile.

The mayor stepped forward and took Hannah's arm. "Come, dear. Let's get you in outta the sun for a cup of tea."

Hannah, Charlotte and many of her friends entered the hotel.

She felt like a queen holding court. Cage, Mitch, Byron, Charlotte, Bernice and Carter all sat with her at one table. The other brides and Nellie served refreshments to the rest of the people, who had crowded into the dining room. Weary but happy, Hannah accepted well wishes as people dropped by the table.

Bernice suggested Hannah use her room to lie down for an hour or two before supper.

She looked to Cage beside her. "That's a good idea. I'm going to check on the horses at the livery and see my friend Nickolai."

"Will you come back here for supper?" She didn't want to be parted for long.

"Yes." He gave her a loving smile.

"All right then." They squeezed hands under the table and Hannah rose.

When she finished her sleep, Nellie had a bath prepared for her. She luxuriated in the scented bubbles as the tension and fear of the time of her captivity started to leave her.

Cage didn't seem to be concerned by the fact she'd been alone with two men for a long time. Relieved, she crossed off that worry. The brides and Charlotte had readily accepted her too.

As she finished rinsing off, she thought she would just have to face any town's women who chose to look down their noises at her. She got out of the tub and primped for her supper with Cage and the others.

Upon entering the dining room, she was surprised and delighted. Nellie and the brides had gone all out to provide a celebration with all the trimmings for her homecoming.

Cage stood with a group of men that included the mayor, the minister, and his friend Nickolai, the blacksmith. The men including Cage had spiffed up for the occasion. She walked over to them with a big smile on her face. Cage introduced her to Nickolai.

Nellie directed them to a head table. "The damsel with her heroes," Nellie teased as she showed them to their places.

While they enjoyed the wonderful meal, Hannah saw a change in the relationship between Cage, Mitch and Byron. She noticed less tension and animosity in Cage toward his brother and father. Even Charlotte and Byron seemed tolerant toward each other.

As they lingered over dessert, Hannah thanked God for the changes He had made while she was gone.

He had answered her prayers.

Cage rose to his feet beside her. Mitch clinked his glass to get everyone's attention.

Hannah wrung her hands in her lap as Cage knelt on one knee before her. His dark eyes smiled. Her breath caught while her heart beat a happy tattoo in her chest.

"Hannah Wall, will you do me the honor of becoming my wife?"

She gasped as the lie she had been living hit her. Tears stung her eyes and throat as she gathered her wits to give this poor, dear man an answer.

"No, Hannah Wall cannot marry you."

She heard several people gasp.

Mitch stepped forward and placed a supportive hand on Cage's shoulder. Cage, his eyes wide hung his head.

Lord, please forgive me for the lie I told. Afraid Harland could trace her she had changed her name to Wall.

"But Hannah Walters would be delighted to marry you."

Cheers rang throughout the room and the women clapped. Mitch patted Cage on the back.

Cage thought his heart had stopped when he heard the word, No. His mind seemed to shut down and he no longer heard what she said.

All of his hopes and dreams crashed into the pit of despair in which he had lived since he had resigned himself to Hannah being gone for good. His pulse thundered in his ears. He couldn't hear what she said next. Despair and regret washed over him in waves weakening his knees and he thought he might pass out.

He had forgotten the ring in his hand. It floated in his line of sight as if in mid-air between them.

Hannah's hands clutched at the cloth the ring sat on and he wondered why. Was she going to fling it in his face? Then Mitch's voice broke through. What had he said?

"Give her the ring."

What for?

So she could toss it at his feet?

Then Nickolai's voice came from somewhere near his other shoulder. "She said yes, man. Give her the ring before she changes her mind."

The room erupted in laughter and the fog that gripped Cage's mind lifted a little.

She said yes?

Could it be true?

His eyes lifted from the box to Hannah's sweet face. A smile of happiness and acceptance shone down upon him.

"Yes Cage. I said, yes."

"Give her the ring." Mitch's voice prompted.

"Put it on her finger," Nickolai urged.

With hands that shook and equally shaking legs, he stood and placed the ring on her finger.

"Kiss her, boy." Byron's baritone rang out from nearby.

Mitch gave him a nudge.

Thunderous applause and cheers echoed as Hannah melted into his arms.

Her petite frame clung to his as she offered her lips for his kiss. Kept short for the sake of remaining proper, it held the promise of many more heated ones to come.

As Cage broke the kiss, Bernice's rosewater perfume assailed his senses. She almost ripped Hannah out of his arms for a hug.

Byron toasted the happy couple with his water glass from the meal. Then people came forward to offer their congratulations.

When Charlotte made her way through the crowd, Cage couldn't hold back his happy tears any longer. The three of them would make a life together on the McCormack land.

After the brides came by to give well wishes, Hannah marvelled at the turn her life had taken.

From a nurse in Boston to a bride on a prairie ranch.

From a frightened girl on the run to a young woman prepared to settle down.

Then her thoughts turned to Cage.

From an angry, bitter man to a man reconciled with his family.

From a young man whose attitude almost guaranteed he'd never marry to a contented man ready to become a groom.

Chapter Twenty Three

Both Hannah and Cage's lives' tapestries had many knots and tangles in the side they could see. But God in his wisdom had woven a beautiful picture on the side He could see.

On the day they married, the edges would weave together and the tapestry would become one solid picture of God's design.

He would continue to weave perhaps with some children in the portrait, probably with many more knots and tangles.

But if they continued to pray and trust in Him, it would be a glorious picture worth the pain and problems that occurred in the weaving.

Made in the USA
Charleston, SC
22 August 2014